Love's Deceit

By

Janine L. Coaxum

Janine Coaxum

Cover Designs by
Daria J. B. Nesmith
GreeneHouse Media
www.greenehousemedia.com
Barron Steward
www.barronsteward.com

Interior Layout and Design by
Brian Young
www.yd-design.com ~ brian@yd-design.com

For booking information please send an email to jlcoaxum@gmail.com.

Love's Deceit is a work of fiction. Names, characters, places, and incidents are products of the author's imagination or used fictitiously. Any resemblance to actual events, locales, or persons, living or dead, is entirely coincidental.

ISBN: 978-0-9800071-1-4
To order additional copies, please visit
www.amazon.com Keyword: Janine Coaxum

Editorial consideration by Treesa Elam-Respass, Tracy L. Scott, and Coffeedreamz Ink, LLC

Dedication

I dedicate this book to boredom.
Thanks for the inspiration.

Special Thanks

I'd like to thank Shenethia Hebert for her inspiration and contribution to this project. I love you, my sister.

Chapter One
The End

"Wake up, my love."

I opened my eyes to complete darkness and found myself struggling...to...breathe. Panic had my heart in my throat. I tried to swallow and realized something was stuffed in my covered mouth. I felt the tape pull my skin. Sweaty tears stung my eyes. Gradually, I became aware of my surroundings.

The space was tight and small. My knees were beginning to ache because my body was bent at an angle. I attempted to roll slowly from my left side onto my stomach, but my face was slammed onto a floor. My wrists were bound behind my back, so I tried to use my shoulders to reposition myself and ended up in a more awkward position. Then I realized more tape was wound around my upper torso. *Relax and breathe*, I repeated to myself. However, every time I tried to take a deep breathe through my nose I panicked even more because the tape around my mouth almost covered my nostrils. I couldn't think. I couldn't...think. My head was pounding. *Where was I? What happened?*

My body was jarred up and slammed back down repeatedly. I let out a muffled and hoarse scream with each movement.

As more sweat ran into my eyes, I squinted to focus on a speck of light that made its way through the darkness. *I was in a car! I was in the trunk of a car!* I stayed still and listened to the clunky, but solid engine. I rolled around in the trunk as the car went over potholes and around corners without slowing down. Every inch of my body ached from the relentless and unforgiving contact it made with the hard, cold surface of the trunk. With each labored breath I took, new smells assaulted my senses. Smells of mold, grease and dirt---old car smells.

When? What was I doing? Where was I? I was trying to remember my day's events to no avail. The car stopped abruptly, and my body jolted. It was torture.

A car door creaked open and then slammed shut. I couldn't hear anything. No traffic, no footsteps. Nothing. The silence was deafening. It became sheet music for my pain. The thump in my head was the bass line. My song of pain built with each sharp note from my neck to my shoulders. My hips and knees joined in the chorus, and my breathing added a dark grey harmony.

I heard footsteps. They were light and shuffled. Scared, I listened intently. I struggled to breathe even more.

The trunk flew open and a bright light hit my face and hurt my eyes. Instinctively, I turned my head and closed my eyes again. I was becoming sick to my stomach, and my mouth began to water as the taste of vomit emerged.

Tug! Tug! Tug! I was being pulled out of the trunk by someone singing.

"Later, later, later, later. Sharlotte said she would talk to me later. Suddenly the room was full of haters, full of folks who would love to date her," the voice sang.

More tugging brought me closer to dispensing the contents of my stomach. I tried hard not to vomit because my mouth was still covered. I would have choked to death.

Breathe, Sharlotte. Breathe! I told myself.

My legs and bare feet were exposed to cold, wet air. A combination of excruciating pain, bright light, nausea and fear were my glue. I was stuck. I tried not to lose my mind as I considered the possibility of what I might see if I were to open my eyes. My back was scraped on the edge of the trunk and then my entire body hit the ground.

I passed out.

***

I regained consciousness after what seemed a week to hear someone singing again.

"Later, later, later, later. Sharlotte said she would talk to me later..."

I couldn't make out the voice.

"Wake up my love. Wake up and smile at me," the stranger spoke.

I so desperately hoped I was dreaming. My body was numb and I couldn't open my eyes wide enough to make out where I was. I tried to speak, but not a bit of air would pass through my lips. I thought to sit up, get up, stand up, and run away. All I could do was listen.

The voice spoke again, low and raspy. Was it a man or a woman?

"Wake up my love. Wake up! I have you now and I'm not going to let anything break us a part. *Later, later,....*" The voice trailed off and then I heard a loud crash.

I took a deep breath. Pain electrified my body and I opened my mouth. It wasn't stuffed or taped anymore. I slowly opened one eye at a time. I left my mouth open and took in the dust-filled air that made me cough. I was finally able to scream. It came out an airy whimper.

One single light from what seemed like a garage hung from the ceiling. The bulb flickered and with every sputter I saw a new scene, a new shadow. I tried to sit up and moved my left arm. My fingers ached. My elbows were bruised.

"You're awake, Dear Sharlotte," my enemy spoke to me again.

I cut my eyes all around the room and caught a glimpse of a shadow to my right. My head pounded. I closed my eyes, hoping to wake from this nightmare.

"Sharlotte, I have plans for us. I'll clean you up. I'll comb your hair and put some of that perfume on you that smells so good." I still couldn't make out the voice.

I heard footsteps draw closer. I opened my eyes to a shadow hovering over me. The person causing me so much pain was standing right in front of me with a hooded sweat shirt. I still couldn't see a face.

"I'll clean you up, Sharlotte, and make sure you look real nice once you're dead. It won't hurt, I promise."

Dead? DEAD! Once I was dead? My mind raced.

This monster who hovered over me pulled out a knife and cut my left wrist. I couldn't move. The right was next. I tried to

8

scream and felt air passing through my lips, but there was only a hissing sound. The blood running over my hand was cool.

I blinked over and over, realizing this was no nightmare. This was real. I was living the end of my life. I was awake and dying.

I opened my mouth and took in a deep breathe, only to halfway inhale just before the knife reached my throat. I had no more strength, no more energy. I was fading. That light hanging from the ceiling dimmed. My perfectly matching slits, perpendicular to the bottom of my palms, were draining the life out of me. Just as I prepared to close my eyes forever, the cold hand touched my throat. One last slit was made and my soul slipped away.

Chapter Two
The Beginning

"You too good to ride with us simple folk?"

I sat restlessly at my little desk, in my little cubicle, tapping my foot, waiting. I can't freakin' wait for five o'clock. I need to go on a walk, do something to relax my mind. I wasn't stressed, wasn't bored, just tired of being so damn *blah*. Five o'clock couldn't come fast enough.

"Goodnight, Cynthia. See you tomorrow!" I sang to my coworker in the office across the hall from my cubicle, and I headed down the hall to the elevator.

Ugh! Here come 11 million damn people. Why do people walk up to the damn elevator, see the damn button lit up and push the damn button again? Shut up Sharlotte, you know you've done it too.

The elevator doors open. Too many damn people, I'll wait for another one. I stand off to the side while 7, 8, 9, 10, 11 people all pile into the elevator like it was the 3:10 to Yuma. I notice a few eyes looking my way as the doors close, as if to say, "you too good to ride with us simple folk?" My eyes reply, "Why yes, I am!" As soon as the light on the elevator button goes out, I pushed the button again. This time only two or three people show up. *Cool. That's better.*

The elevator doors open and all get on. There is some hesitation as to who is going to push the button for the first floor. I am farthest away. Somebody, anybody…damn it, "I GOT IT!" I spat irritably, as I made my way past one gentleman who was looking up at the display, waiting for the elevator to begin its decent. I let out a huff as I thought to myself, I need to take a walk, BAD! Walking helps to clear my mind and ease my spirit. Walking calms my soul, keeps my weight down and keeps me from looking like a hot ghetto mess.

The elevator doors opened and we all got off. I swiped my badge, listened for the chime and headed out the door into the basement of the four deck parking garage. The smell of cigarette smoke immediately assaulted my nostrils and just about gave me a headache. I hate those freakin' Nicotine Pirates! They're always standing one inch beyond the "NO SMOKING WITHIN 50 FEET" sign. They're always begging other people who come out to smoke for a cigarette. Hence, the name Nicotine Pirates.

Why the HELL would you come outside to smoke and you ain't got no cigarettes? By this time of day, I can't wait to get home, change my clothes and go for a walk to relax in some fresh crisp air. While making my way through the lowest level of the parking garage to my car, I pulled out my PDA and dialed up my best friend Tara. I immediately got a connection, but just barely, the basement of the parking garage got crappy reception.

"Hey girl! What's good? Naw, I'm JUST leavin work. I know it's like three minutes after five, you ain't gotta tell me! I'm getting in my car RIGHT now. How was your day?" Blah blah blah. Tara and I go on about nothing as usual.

We chat, make jokes and both laugh. This is how most of our "after work" conversations go. I call Tara everyday when leaving work and our conversations always encompassed the same dialogue. Funny thing is, we never get tired of it.

I got into my Mercedes CLS 500 and started the engine. As I checked my rear view mirror, I noticed someone standing about 200 feet to my right. I described the person to Tara as I checked left to right for oncoming traffic. I was nowhere near paranoid, but the way the person just kind of stood there, creeped me out. Whoever it was wasn't getting in or out of any vehicle, not looking for any vehicle in particular and certainly wasn't gabbing on a cell phone like I was. *Weird*, I thought. I backed out of my parking space, entertaining questions from Tara, and drove towards the garage exit.

Dr. Tara Steele, my best friend, is a professional woman, a Psychiatrist. The divorced mother of two little girls, Kayla and Shauna, Tara is busy, busy, busy. Yet and still, she makes time for good friendship and good conversation, and I loved her for that. I wouldn't trade her or her two girls for the world. I wrapped up my conversation with Tara and made a quick left onto New York Avenue, fighting to merge with assholic drivers all the way. *Assholic* might not be a word, but guess what? It is today. I left the radio off and preferred to drive in silence, listening to engines and raggedy stereo systems. The entire drive home was filled with noise.

I can't wait to go for a walk so that I can hear everything and nothing all at once. To be on two feet and wings in the same stride. To be free. I'm almost there. Traffic light. Another traffic light. Red to green.

I thought to myself, *"Why don't the lights here in the U.S. go from red to yellow to green like some of the ones in Europe? It's not like all the impatient road demons haven't already taken their foot off the brake any damn way. And for the ones who aren't paying attention because they're texting (like me), it's a courteous heads up. It's Hey, lady. The light's fixin' ta turn green so press send or finish your text at the next light.* The light turns green.

"OH!" I exhaled, made a left turn, swerved around a car that made a last minute decision to turn left, then picked up speed as I charged out of the pack of cars just barely doing 20 miles an hour. What the hell? I'm not admitting to road rage, but come on! 20 miles an hour. For what? I made a left turn into my luxury apartment home complex and pressed the button to go through the gate, made a left turn and parked. "Ahhhh. Finally home."

I could feel my muscles start to relax as my mind began to unwind. The thoughts running through my head from the day's events slowed down. They never come to a complete halt, just slow down. I got out of my car and noticed an unusual car parked at the far end of the parking lot...an Oldsmobile that had obviously seen its fair share of accidents. Cream in color, the bumper was metal and the areas where it met the frame were rusted through. The visible tires were missing hubcaps and the car was double parked at an angle. That piece of junk will definitely be towed by morning. My thoughts turned back to my plan for the evening.

Janine Coaxum

As I walked through the door of my apartment Cocoa, my Pekingese, awakened in her kennel. I greeted her saying the usual, "Hey, Boo!" and let her out to stretch. She sniffed and snuggled my legs as I hooked her up to her leash.

We took a quick walk to the mailbox, stopping along the way so that Cocoa could mark previously marked territory. I got the usual mail-- junk advertisements, bills--and headed back to my apartment. Once we returned to the apartment, I set out food for Cocoa and changed my clothes while she ate. I was excited about my walk, my journey into freedom. I put my long hair (all real) in a ponytail, threw on my beige Members Only jacket, warm wool black scarf, sweats from my days in the Army and New Balance sneakers.

I walked into the kitchen where Cocoa was eating. She stopped and looked at me. I looked back at her. We looked at each other in silence. "Well, hurry up!", I said breaking that silence. Cocoa snuffed and put her face back in her bowl. Once Cocoa finished, I hooked her up to her leash once more and headed out into to the crisp October air.

This was my first October in Maryland. I was used to southern seasons. Warm winters and hot summers. I took in a deep breath, embracing the smells. I hadn't walked in a good while. Sometimes life got so busy that I forgot to take time out for myself, forgot to pamper myself and to tend to my inner most needs.

Walking was my time out activity and I was way past ready to get back to it. I started out down the side walk of my apartment complex and headed toward the main road. I set out on a two mile walk around the Metro Station.

I relaxed into my steps. Two miles. Wasn't much to me, sometimes not enough but it was better than nothing. Cocoa peed here and there, leaving her scent along the way. I took another deep breath. Fresh cut grass. Exhaust. Water. I took in every smell Maryland had to offer. It smelled like it was going to rain. You can tell by that statement that I'm a southern girl.

I crossed over a two lane divided street that ran past my apartment complex, passed the Metro Station, Strayer University and a Seafarers Union. I made a left at Red Lobster and as I rounded the corner at a good pace, I noticed the beat up Oldsmobile from my apartment complex, driving by slowly. I cut my pace in half and watched as the hoopty continued down the street past me, puttering and rocking, as black smoke came from the tail pipe.

My heart pumping, I continued on. As I came up on a popular BMW dealership, I saw her. She was walking towards me and was at least 50 yards ahead of me. She had a nice, long weave, Yaki 1b probably, sunshades that covered most of her face and lip gloss that was poppin'.

Diva honey was sporting a tan leather mid-length jacket, a white leather skirt and knee high black leather boots. She had a big Louie Vuitton bag clutched by her side and the baddest stroll I've seen in a while. I almost tripped trying to get an eyeful. As I approached her, I looked down at the ground. I wanted to watch her walk, track the sway in her hips. I wanted to look at her, but not for so long that she would feel uncomfortable, so I waited. I timed it.

Just as we approached each other, I looked up long enough to get in an eye full. I noticed her breasts. They were jungle breasts. She wore a shear leopard print shirt under her tan leather jacket and under the sheerness of her leopard print shirt was a shiny

15

black bra. A miracle bra, at least a cup size too small. I remember her breasts were smushed and squeezed under those spots, like an elephant hiding behind a bush. Jungle breasts, wild sho nuff.

I smiled; she smiled. It was that fake *"Hey. Yeah Hey to you, too"* smile, but nothing more was required.

As we passed by each other, I glanced at the BMW lot and noticed that Diva Honey had an audience; a gentleman standing at the backdoor of his car watched her as she switched down the side walk. His mouth hung wide open. *Brother, don't I know!* I turned my attention back to the path set ahead of me and tried to refocus, but her scent lingered in the air. She smelled like fresh Italian leather. Clean and expensive. She looked luscious. She smelled soft and clean and her smell lingered with me for at least another five minutes after I passed her.

I eased back into my groove, taking in what I pleased of my environment and tossing the rest aside. Cocoa was in full trot. Her short legs were keeping pace with my steps. Her head bobbing up to sniff cool fresh air and down to explore new and familiar scents in the grass; we walked. Just as I turned left around a corner, a tall, thin man came out of a building, talking quietly on his cell phone. Cocoa and I crossed a parking lot. So did he. We hit the sidewalk to continue our journey around the Metro and so did he. I slowed my pace to put some distance between us. I don't need some total stranger thinking we can get buddy buddy and then before you know it, somebody has talked away 30 minutes of your life that you can't ever get back. His long legs and my short steps put plenty of space between us in no time.

Now back to my groove. I took in the air which had gotten chillier than when I started out. Still, good. Still, fresh. I checked behind me to see if I had anymore unwelcomed company. I did not. Since my move from Georgia, I hadn't been consistent with my walking. Between work, side jobs, getting settled and used to the area, I hadn't been out.

On these walks I'd get ideas, think of lyrics to songs and explore my creative side. It was wonderful to have that back. Of everything creative I've come up with on these walks, love was always the main theme. Love.

I was fascinated by love and our expression of it. The way in which we manifest it, decipher its language, misunderstand it and misinterpret it baffles me. Love. We love, but deceive each other in it. Surely this is not the way it's intended to be, but nevertheless, this is how we do it. I was on my own quest for love, open to any suggestions and taking applications.

It was on this particular walk that it hit me. I hadn't been honest with my love. I'd said I loved people, but wasn't always true to that love. I either held back for fear of hurting the other person or let it go for fear of being hurt by people. Either way, I was ruining any chance I had at truly loving anyone from the very beginning. It was at that moment that I decided to love truly. The next encounter, chance, or opportunity that I had at loving someone, I was going explore to its fullest potential. I had decided at that moment to love that person as truly as I possibly could. Some might refer to me as the classic angry black woman, but I really wasn't.

I was lonely and I had only recently admitted this fact to myself. I was in my mid 30s and though I wouldn't change my life for the world, I was ready for more. I realized that I needed a lesson in love. I just hadn't figured out what that lesson was, until I met him. Thus began my love story. Of all the love stories ever told, this one is most important. This love story has a lesson to be learned. We are all so very familiar with the deception discovered through love. What happens when love's deceit is explored? Let loose and let go.

Chapter Three
Sharlotte Swanson

"Who else could it be?"

Who am I? Allow me to further introduce myself. I'm the baddest woman you'll ever wanna meet. I'm street smart, business savvy, I.N.D.E.P.E.N.D.E.N.T. Do you know what that means? I look like a model chick. Ok, I'm lying about most of that, except for being independent. Who do I need to be in order to be someone in this world? Why can't I just be me, Sharlotte Swanson: daughter of divorced and remarried parents, with three step sisters and two half brothers, who I spent all of maybe three years around, collectively?

I'm the best friend to some of the most diverse and talented women you ever wanna meet. I am Sharlotte, the chick with a master's degree, no kids, a mortgage, a baller's car payment, and several jobs. That's me. Sharlotte Swanson. Who else COULD it be?

Since the move, I've been on the prowl. It seems as if there isn't a decent man in sight! Don't get it twisted: I've got plenty of men to choose from. I've had tons of men in the past, a couple from the past still on the side, but no Mr. Right. Not even a Mr. Right Now. To expedite my search for Mr. Right, I've turned to the Internet. My best friend, Tara, says that using the Internet to screen men may 'cause a problem for me down the road. I tried to explain to her that I'm no stranger to the Internet dating scene. Let me explain.

The World Wide Web is a web indeed. With so many social network websites, a sistah could date, get married, have sperm sent to her house, birth a kid nine months later and then divorce the sperm donor without ever leaving the computer. This thing is serious. I believe I was hooked to it. I was addicted you might even say, addicted to dating web sites.

These sites offered the anonymity of screening your potential mate, cut buddy or whoever you desired. They're mostly the same. Some you pay money, others are free. You set up an account, create a page, put up a few pictures. Say something simple and then it's ready, set, flirt!

Click! Click! Click! You could royally screw up the wheel on a mouse without even trying. So many pages to visit. So many faces, half naked bodies and smiles and tongues. There were so many men licking their lips, holding their manhood and claiming to want *"A woman who's got her own and don't need mine."*

That seemed to be the commonality amongst most of the profiles. The same underlying theme: *I'm a good man looking for a good woman.* What they should be saying is:
Man whore looking for next victim. Will sex you quickly and leave you sickly.

Some profiles actually try honesty and I bet it gets them the cookies just as well. These are profiles of men(and women) who run the gambit. You have your married men looking for swingers and flings...some are smart enough to request discretion. Then you have your "Involved/Partners" who have *"in"*significant others whose geographic locations are always questionable. They don't know what in the world they want. You've got your gigolo's, pretty boys who are so empty inside. It's scary. I'm talking nothing upstairs and nothing in the heart. Just plain empty.

Rarely do you run across a decent and attractive man on these sites. They are out there, but they are hidden. They are not flashy, don't talk trash or boast about how they lay the pipe. They're like me, just looking for some decent conversation and enjoying the circus act in the meantime. I think that's what kept me coming back for more.

True, the aforementioned is what often made me delete my profile and leave it alone, but in the end, I just kept coming back for more. Sick ain't it? Don't judge; just read.

So back to why I didn't have a man for the longest. I can say a lot, but what it boils down to is this: I was open to a relationship, but very particular about its characteristics. I believed then and still believe now, if I am going to honestly love someone, that person needs to meet some simple standards.

It's nothing complicated, promise. I am interested in a man who has the same things to offer me that I have to offer him. (Clearing my throat) THE LIST:

1. He must be educated ....preferably not by the streets.
2. Never been married
3. Have no children
4. Good credit (score of at least 500)
5. Have a full head of hair (bald by choice for whatever reason is acceptable)
6. Have and be able to maintain a car (including the car payment)

7. Have a good job (a career is always a plus)

8. Live alone (a roommate for financial purposes is acceptable and understandable... Times are hard! Why not save money? That means there's more to spend on me! Just kidding, but only not really)

9. Like animals (Cocoa is a ride or die dog, where I go, she goes)

10. Not be clingy, needy, verbally abusive or overly physically aggressive (that includes sexually...who the hell told ya'll rough guys that was sexy)

11. Have SOME money and know how to manage it.

12. Last, but certainly not least, love his family and friends

See? Not complicated at all. Unfortunately, once I get past the first two items on the agenda, the pickins are damn slim. The men that are left at the end of the list are ugly, fat, bourgie, into exotic chicks or gay.

See my plight?. Is this coming in any clearer? See why I was single for so long? Back in that time, like Maya Angelou, still...I rise.....in the mornings on my day off and surf these freakin' social sites. Looking. Not necessarily for love, but for something. Someone. Just talking about it makes me ill.

Who am I? I am Sharlotte Swanson: Hairdresser extraordinaire, poet, Military Veteran, songwriter, singer, babysitter, counselor, therapist and sexual beast. I'm a comedian, but only to some. I'm sarcastic but never rude to others. Then again, I'm soft and sincere to the like. Overall,

Janine Coaxum

I'd have to say I am a butterfly. I determine the proximity in which you admire my beauty then flutter away at a moment's notice. Pay close attention to my colors.

Chapter Four
Georgia

"Damn Girl, THINK!"

It was August and I had decided to go down to Georgia to visit Tara and the girls. Tara's oldest girl, Kayla, had joined the cheerleading squad, so I had to make a special trip down for her first game of the season. She did such a wonderful job. They were cute! The team colors were royal purple and bright green. Kayla wore a purple sleeveless top and a white fly away skirt trimmed in the team colors. Her hair was in a single ponytail atop her head with a multitude of ribbons tied to it.

"Who the hell put all them ribbons in Kayla's ponytail like that?" I asked joking with her mom. "I hope whoever did it is going to be around to get that mess out!". Tara and I both knew it was the cheerleading coach, little Miss Rich Lady, who just so happened to be the wife of the football coach.

"They know good and well those ribbons get tangled in their hair," I complained.

Tara wrinkled her face, shook her head and told me the cheerleading coach had insisted they wear at the very least three. With all the jumping around they did, Kayla was going to have a time getting that ribbon out without shedding a few tears. I thought it was funny.

As the game concluded, parents packed their kids and equipment in their cars as they yakked on cell phones, hollered across scores of screaming boys and girls and simultaneously multitasked. Tara and I were joining in the dance when my cell phone rang. It was my "caller" ringing.

I answered, annoyed, "Sharlotte Swanson.
Who the hell is this? Get the hell outta here, STOP CALLING ME! Lose my freakin' number!"
END.

As Kayla and her younger sister Shauna buckled themselves in, I pulled Tara from the driver's side door a few feet to the rear of her Maserati.

I inhaled and then let out, "I'm just saying!. I've had this telephone number for 11 million years. There is no way one stupid freak is going to harass and press me into changing my number. Everybody has this number. All of my
family, friends, colleagues and people from years ago who I'll probably never see again, but can still freakin' call me. This is some bull crap."

"Sharlotte, who was that?" Tara asked.

"Girl, I haven't the slightest idea. For real... Why are you lookin' at me like that? I said I didn't know!"

My girl let in on me. "You do know. You know who you gave your number to. It's a cell phone number. It ain't like they got our cell phone numbers listed in a cell phone book somewhere. You gave your number to one of those Internet guys didn't you? Uh huh....and if you didn't, you gave it to somebody who gave it to somebody else, who gave it to one of those Internet guys. Sharlotte, you gonna mess up one good time one day and it's gonna be a wrap. I'm talkin' *all she wrote*." You gotta be more careful!"

"Damn, Mom. Are you done?"

"No. And another thing, you don't live close anymore. So what if something popped off? Then what? Everybody you know lives 10 ½ hours away. Damn, girl, THINK! I can't just leave my kids and hop on the highway to come check on your ass should you get into some mess!...Now...I'm done."

I love Tara. Really I do. I love my best friend more than my dog. More than I love taking walks. I love her almost more than I love music. Almost. But damn she can hit a nerve. She's right though.

It had been four months since I moved from Georgia to Maryland and I was still getting the calls. With the revolution of the cell phone, I stopped paying for a home phone. It was a waste of good money to have two different telephone numbers when everyone called the cell phone number first anyway. You never knew if I was home or out, so my cell phone rang first, consistently. Truth be told, I hadn't had a home telephone number in the last five years.

The calls started in early June and I'd been receiving them off and on. Somebody would ring me from an unknown number and the number would be different every time. Normally don't answer unknown or blocked numbers, but since the move, a lot of the business related calls I needed to take were unknown or blocked numbers. In an effort to accommodate my new line of work, I tried to answer numbers with (DC, Maryland, Virginia) DMV area codes.

Janine Coaxum

What do I do you wonder? Why don't I have a work cell number you wonder? Well long story short, I have several jobs. The IRS only knows of one. The other jobs include, but are not limited to: consulting, singing, braiding (synthetic and natural hair) and tutoring. So, my cell phone is a catch all, business and pleasure.

That first call, a month after I got to Maryland, wasn't anything big. I paid it no attention. I was leaving an orientation session at my new 9-to-5 when my cell phone chimed. It was an unknown number. I answered, "Sharlotte Swanson." All I heard was a muffled rustling of papers or clothes against the phone. It almost sounded like someone had been pocket dialing. Then I heard them say something. It was very low and I almost didn't make it out. I still wonder if I heard right. *I love those shoes.*

I simply hung up. I didn't say a word. I didn't acknowledge that I had even heard what was said. I had hoped that by not fceding whatever motivated my caller, the person would stop. Lose interest. Get bored with me not playing along and move on to someone or something else. Not the case. Not my luck.

Two days after I had received the first call, my caller rang me again. I was in the middle of putting up groceries on a warm Saturday afternoon when my phone chimed. With Avelon Organics Peppermint shampoo in one hand and Good Karma Organic Rice Dream in the other, I leaned over my purse to see if the screen on my PDA was visible. It wasn't.

My phone chimed again. I hurriedly put the Good Karma Organic Rice Dream in the freezer and set the Avelon shampoo down on the counter. Dug through my purse, found my phone, looked at the number. It was a D.C. area code, 202.

I answered, *"Sharlotte Swanson"*

"Mmmmmmm, I smell you from here. You smell so damn luscious," the caller said. Silence from me...again.

"I hear you breathing. I imagine the rise and..."
END.

I hung up and continued to put away groceries. It's going to sound strange, but I still thought nothing of it. I didn't think back about whether I had crossed anyone. I didn't wonder if it had been someone from one of those social web site interactions. I just dismissed it like so many other things that didn't make me no never mind.

Of course, I told Tara about it. Not the first time it happened, but I called her right after that second call in June. At first she thought it was funny. Hell, I thought it was funny. Then Tara started in with her devil's advocate spiel. Talking about all the websites and profiles and me "putting myself out there" by having pictures up and what not. Making me think. Making me wonder. Questioning why someone had decided to harass me since the move. I quickly shut that down with my opposing argument of "sometimes there is no why." It's supported by the "Shit Happens Theory", a theory that speaks to occurrences or events that cannot be explained. It's one of my favorites.

The conversation shifted to nonsensical blah blah blah and we laughed some more, then got off the phone. That was the end of June. July, no calls. August, no calls. End of August, school starts, calls start. What's really hood! Does this piece of work have kids, run a summer camp or something? I couldn't figure it out. Coincidence? Or "Shit Happens" Theory.

Chapter Five
Dr. Tara Steele

"Makin It Do What It Do"

Buzz. Vibrate. Buzz. Pause. Buzz. Vibrate. Buzz. The alarm on my phone goes off. At the same time, I roll over to get snuggled in my bed. I think to myself, *I just got in the bed and here this damn alarm clock goes.* I leisurely drag my tired butt out of bed, hoping that by some fluke I accidentally set the clock and it was Saturday morning. Instead, it was really 5:50 a.m. Tuesday morning, August 26th. Damn, no such luck. Might as well motivate and make it do what it do. Time waits for no one.

As I turn the corner of the dark hallway in my two story, $300,000 dollar home, a pair of tiny shoes and a couple of those Micky D's happy meal toys unhappily greet me. You know, the one's that when you step on them and make you want to curse the dumb individual that came up with it. You want to curse yourself even more for not cooking and resorting to the Happy Meal Diner's club for what, in essence, amounts to you paying $3 for a toy that cost three pennies? A stupid toy that your child will never play with again once the last French fry is consumed.

I call out, *"Girls get up or you're gonna be late."* I hear no one move an inch. In a louder, but compassionate (or maybe just tired) tone, I call out once again, *"Girls, GET UP NOW!"* Kayla, my oldest daughter who's 10, rolls herself to a sitting position while Shauna, my youngest who's five going on 30, barely moves.

In the most loving tone I can muster up at 6 a.m., I speak to Shauna, "If I have to tell you one more time it's going to be you and me chick." She manages to roll out of the bed. As I walk out of their room, I think to myself...*another day in the life of mommyhood.*

"If I could sleep for 30 more minutes life would be good," I bargain with myself.

I plop back down on the bed, I turn on the television and turn to the local news to catch a glimpse of the weather and drama in the world. I'm comfortably garbed in my unattractive wrinkled T-shirt and boy shorts. My zone was interrupted when I heard yelling.

"Hurry up and move out of the way!" Kayla screamed at her sister. A river of tears poured from cranky Shauna's eyes. Poor baby, she's not a morning person at all. Damn, here we go again.

"Shauna! Go into my bathroom and brush your teeth."

As I am witnessing another dose of the "I hate my sister" saga, my attention is turned to the television. I hear that another soldier is believed to have murdered his wife. Why couldn't he have just divorced her? Why did he have to take her life?

Right before I strip to wash the sleep funk from my body, I do a time check and remind Shauna to get dressed and not to get back in the bed.

"Tell your sister to hurry up in the bathroom and put the iron up when she is done," I said and then went into the shower, but not before turning on the radio for some motivation.

The water feels superior flowing down my 5'11" medium statured body. As the water warms up to a steamy temperature, I let it run freely over my back and down my dark chocolate thighs. I think about what it would be like to be a porn star in a shower scene.

I squeeze my thighs together and rub my already hard nipples. I shower with Cream Ribbons body wash. After I squeeze some on my puff I lather up. Circles and lines, parallel and perpendicular. Up my thighs and down between my legs. Slowly, around my full breasts. Damn, my breast still look great! Even after two kids. Lucky me. The steam from my hot oasis embraces me and tantalizes me. Teases me. I want to stay in it forever.

I rinse and moan as I prop my leg on the side of the tub so that I can indulge in a little self-pleasure before taking on the problems of the world. Short bursts of screaming from the kitchen downstairs bring me back to reality. Note to self: Thank the genius builders for putting my bathroom over the kitchen. I can hear the girls through the vent. I sigh. Kayla and Shauna...at it again. I angrily put my leg down, turn off the water and grab for my towel, because this session is definitely over. To be continued...

I think to myself, *Dollar to a dime they are arguing over who gets to pour the cereal and who gets to pour the milk.*

I reluctantly dry off and hang my towel. If I have to, I'll leave my steamy spa to make peace, with my peace maker if need be, but not before I go through my ritual of "divafying" myself. I must continue to hold on to the last thread of hope that I am a sexy woman, not just the chick that slaughters the pig, brings home the bacon, fries it up and serves it with a smile. The mantras and frequent pep talks I give myself are the glue that holds me together.

Pep talks that consist of reminders like, No man wants to see a good-looking woman, smell her orgasmic perfume that works so well with her body chemistry, only to caress her body and have her feel like sandpaper. Just as I complete my ritual of lotions and crèmes, my cell phone rings. (Ringtone by Katy Perry: *I kissed a girl and I liked it.....taste of her cherry ChapStick*). Sharlotte. I giggled at our ringtone for each other. It was Sharlotte's idea of course.

I answered, "Hey girl! Good morning! ...Nothing, getting the girls and myself together, you know, makin' it do what it do!" That's my catchall phrase.

We chat for only a moment more and pledge to call each other after we get going. That's what we do pretty much every morning. Things never deviate from that course of events, at least not by more than two or three hours. If I didn't hear anything from that loud mouth Sharlotte for 24 hours, I'd know something wasn't right. I put down my cell phone and grab my underwear.

While putting on my bra and blouse I heard a crash. As I continue to make progress, I hear the girls screaming at each other. With a deep sigh, I grab the belt and head downstairs.

Chapter Six
The World Wide "Shar"lotte's Web

"Individuals hide their true selves for fear of being judged."

Google. It might just be the greatest thing ever to grace the Internet. Society has even created a "catch all" phrase that has become the complete and utter answer to every question imaginable...Google it. You wanna know how to make chocolate chip cookies? Google it.

You need to find the nearest Wal-mart, Google it. Hell, you want pictures of Omar Tyrese? Google it, Image Search. Need a map of your neighborhood? Google it, Google Earth. Kind of scary, right?

They can use satellite imagery to show your address. You can even see some backyards, dog house and all. Crackhead on the corner, old lady crossing the street, 5 year olds outside on the playground pickin' their noses...ok, maybe I'm exaggerating, but it's some good (but scary) technology. So this is where I begin. I'm looking for websites that host Internet dating sites, so I Google it. Up come thousands of results. Per my search criteria, "Meet Black Singles Now", "BPDate", and "Black World" are the top three results, so I start there.

The first, "Meet Black Single Now", turns out to be a site that has nothing but ads and links on it. You've got to be careful with those because they are the ones that will have you sitting in front of your computer, wondering where the multiple pop-up screens of naked white women spreading themselves wide keep coming from.

I hit the back button and click the next link, "Black People Date". It looks legit. Damn, they want money. It's one of those sites that will let you look, but not play unless you pay. I'm not that hard up for entertainment, so I move on.

Hit the back button. I click on the third link, "Black World". Here we go. This site is free. I do free. Me and free can ride all day, every day. I select the link to start an account.

Personal Information: Name: Sharlotte Swanson

Location: Noneofyourbusiness, Somewhere

Zip Code: 20010

Birthday: 01011977 (Yes. People, I'm thirty something)

Click **here** *to build your personal page.* Ok, now the fun really begins. *Upload a picture.* At this point, I'm thinking back on when the last time was I took a good picture. It's been a minute. I'd just moved to Maryland, got a new job, new place, new car, new attitude and a new haircut. I decide it's time to break out the digital camera and take some new pictures of myself.

1. Fix my hair.
2. Put on some Mac lip gloss.
3. Set the timer. Pose, flash. Hmmmmm, that one's crap. Delete.
4. Add more light to the room. Set the timer. Pose, flash. Better.

Twenty minutes and 35 pictures later, I pop out the memory card and insert it into my computer. *Click* **here** *to upload a photo.* I browse through and select only the best ones, about four. *Upload successful!*

The only thing left to do is design my page. I pick a modest background, fill out the *About Myself* questionnaire then click the "*Go To My Page* link. Ah! I like it. Cool!

Now it's time to browse other members. I select the characteristics of who I want to see: I am a <u>Woman</u> seeking <u>Men</u> between the ages of <u>30</u> and <u>40</u>. Located within <u>30</u> miles of me...Search. Search Results...ugh!

Ten members meet your search criteria.

Why am I NOT surprised? I giggled as I scanned down the page. The screen names for some of these profiles were ridiculous. Very cliché. Names like Bighard4u, Mike69 and Luv2licku. I giggled even more.

I clicked on the first one to catch my interest, Pete75 . His page came up on my screen and I was immediately turned off. Pete75 was plastered across the upper left corner of my screen, shirtless, wearing a pair of jeans and a belt with one of those oversized, outlandish buckles.

What turned me off? His size B cup man boobs. Then there was his gut. It wasn't a good solid slab of fat. It hung over the top half of that preposterously oversized belt buckle. Oh! There was more! Pete75 had another photo to view. I clicked the *More Photos* link thinking it couldn't be too much worse. I was so wrong. There was Pete75 in almost all of his glory and splendor. He had on a pair of gray bikini men's briefs that were stretched and worn so much they read:

C---a----l---v---i---n---K---

He was blubbery and had peezy chest hairs that spanned his entire upper torso. His package was a complete joke. It looked like he had more beans than frank. The icing on the cake was his white socks...Yeah.

After seeing that, it didn't matter what he had to say. I clicked the back button and selected the next profile of interest. *TonedTone1*. This guy looked halfway decent. An alarm went off when I clicked on his link to *view more photos* and saw that he had uploaded 57 images. Narcissistic? Maybe? I viewed them all anyway.

They were pictures of him, him and more him...old pictures of him when he was clearly much younger. There were pictures of him hiking, biking, motorcycle pimpin', partying and generally living it up. There were a few professional photos. He'd posted pictures of him in front of a pure white backdrop and some on a beach walking at sunset.

One photo in particular sparked my interest. It was a picture of him on a rock near a waterfall in some tropical location. He had on a tan linen shirt that was completely open and white linen pants that had a drawstring tie in the front. Brown sandals adorned his feet. His physique was average. Not too much muscle, but certainly no flab. Athletic. He looked very picturesque. Almost perfect and serene.

His face was a smooth brown with a five o'clock shadow. His head was bald. His eyebrows were thick, his nose sharp, lips full and well oiled. His chin and jaw were strong and perfectly squared off. Damn! He looked good! Wait a minute. This was not the man in all the other photos. I click back and forth, selected several pictures, each one saved in my memory for comparison to another. Why didn't all these qualities come through in the other photographs? Was it me simply not paying attention, as I have a tendency to do? No matter.

I went back to his profile to read if there were any brains behind the operation. Well, look at this. He actually wrote something.

Name: JaRah.

Sign: Cancer. *I don' have luck with cancers.*

He wrote about what he liked to do, which was redundant of his photographs, what he was looking for in a female and to contact him by sending him an e-message if there were any questions. So I did. I clicked the link to compose an e-message and my mind went blank. The cursor blinked and I just sat there, staring at it on my screen. Blinking. There, not there, there, not there.

Truthfully, I didn't have any questions to ask him that were appropriate. I mean he was a total stranger, but yet I felt like I had met him like you would meet someone in the grocery store on the cereal aisle. What I wanted to ask him was, "Which of these pictures were recent and why so many?" I chuckled to myself about why it even mattered and decided to just say hello.
SEND.

I browsed a few more profiles and chuckled at the sheer audacity of some of them while I ate my Good Karma Organic Rice Dream Key lime Pie Flavored non dairy rice ice cream.

Suddenly my Inbox icon lit up. I had an e-message. I clicked the inbox link. Pete75 had sent me an e-message. *What?*

I looked at the options that were posted down the side of my page and there it was: *Member's I've Viewed. Members Who've*

Viewed Me. Damn. This website had a tracking system that let people know who's looked at their profile. Great.

Why didn't I notice that before? I immediately went to *account settings* and clicked the option to b*rowse anonymously* and to a*ppear offline.* I believe that individuals hide their true identity for fear of being judged.

Back to my Inbox. *Pete75 has sent you an e-message!* Another one! Ugh!

I clicked to open the first message. I read it.
"Hey sweetheart. I see you lookin. What's up?" he wrote.

Definitely not YOU! DELETE.
I moved on to the second message. It read: "I see you're online. Don't be a snob, respond!" he wrote. DELETE.

I left my Inbox and went back to the member search page. My Inbox icon lit up again. I clicked the inbox link. He responded!

TonedTone1 has sent you an e-message!

Chapter Seven
JaRah Richmond

"Just 'cause a brotha has an ethnic name doesn't mean nuthin!"

I stood in the chill morning air at the pump thinking to myself, *"Damn! Gas is expensive as a mug."* I had recently received a promotion and decided to upgrade my BMW from a 350 to 750. What the hell was I thinking?

I consider myself a reasonable brotha, not too flashy when it comes to material things. I generally have good business sense and make wise choices with my money, but this economy has taken a steep dive and made penny pinchers squirm at the thought of spending a quarter. I did it any way. I decided to trade in my late model BMW for a new 750. Hell! I deserved it. I worked hard these past seven years handling accounts and saving my firm millions. Last month, they recognized the 60 hours plus a brotha had been putting in. I must have jumped in pay at least $20,000 a year. So, I waited two pay checks. I didn't really see the increase on the first check? I expected that. The second check, oh boy. Now that's what I'm talkin' 'bout!

Once I saw what I was working with, I made up my mind to treat myself to an upgrade. It was October, kinda chilly out, but I had the top down on *Lisa* (my late model) anyhow. *Last ride, baby, last ride.* I hit the beltway and opened her up. Hit a hundred, then crept up to 120 and 130 miles per hour. I slowed down, as traffic was beginning to congest. Too much swerving in and out of lanes would get you picked up on that aggressive driver imaging quick.

I moved from the far left lane, over the six lanes of traffic, to the far right lane and prepared to exit.Once I got off, it was a straight shot to the dealership. I arrived early in the afternoon. I knew I'd be there for atleast five hours. Buying a car takes about that much time, so I took the day off. I planned to take my time.

You have to test drive or rather flirt with a couple of cars and then narrow down the choices.

Run the numbers, send off credit applications, blah,blah, blah.

I parked *Lisa* and went inside. I scanned the room, looking at the salesmen who all looked at me like I was fresh meat. I peeped an older brotha in the back of the showroom, rappin to the receptionist seated behind a counter. You couldn't see much of her because of how high the counter was, but I could tell by the position of her freshly drawn eyebrows, that she was cheesin' hard. That's my man. The playa, the pimp.

I walked towards him. I saw the other salesmen looking my way, but ignored them. I wanted to give this distinguished looking man my business. He resembled my Uncle Q, but his swagger was like that of my father.

The Sales Representative I approached was tall, slender, had salt and pepper hair that connected into a neatly cropped beard. He wore a crisply starched long sleeve, white button-up collared shirt, a blue argyle sweater, khaki colored dress pants and brown Stacy Adams. I recognize that squared toe anywhere. His cuff links were canary yellow to offset the yellow in his blue argyle sweater and matched his yellow bowtie. A cool cat with black lips that told he smoked.

As I approached him, he looked up at me away from the receptionist reluctantly, as if he was just about to get the digits. She continued to smile at him as he turned to me, as if she knew he had to make that money in order for him to get the cookies. I extended my hand and we greeted each other the way black men do.

Sup, my brotha? Slap. Fist. Pound. Tap the shoulder.

I let him know what my interests were and we went from there. As we headed out the showroom, I looked back at the receptionist and saw her peek over the counter.

Her look said, *Go make that money, Daddy!* My Sales Representative's name was Larry, and Larry knew his stuff. He took me through the history of the BMW, even told me a few things about *Lisa* that I didn't know. About six hours and seven models later, I found the one. I found the 750 I was going to treat myself to. It was beginning to be dusk, the air had cooled significantly. I wanted to peruse the lot while Larry printed the paperwork, so I headed back to *Lisa* to get my coat. That's when I saw her. She was walking by the dealership. She was cute. I couldn't really see much other than her round booty and her ponytail bobbin, but I caught her smile. She didn't see me, though. Her smile looked so familiar. I immediately ran through my mental rolodex of women...nope. I drew a blank, but I knew I had seen her somewhere.

She had on army sweat pants, a black scarf and a beige Member's Only jacket! Wow! I started to laugh 'cause I hadn't seen one of those in a minute. Truly a throwback if ever I saw one. She was walking a dog. She was walking the little thing that had a fancy cut. You know how women do their dogs sometimes, bows, perfume and clothes and whatnot. Her dog wasn't like that, just had a fancy cut, a bushy tail. It was a little black dog that pranced and she pranced right behind it. She was moving, really stepping it out when she first caught my eye then she slowed down. I thought at first it was because she saw me and smiled.

Then I saw *her*...this bad chick coming from the opposite direction. She looked like singer Amerie from where I was standing. She had on fresh Italian looking leather, short skirt and her tit-tays were jumping for me! Ooooo-weeee! I held my cool, 'cause that's just how I do, but the first girl...she almost tripped on the sidewalk looking at Mami. I thought it was cute. Kind of like the way freshmen girls look at the senior girls when they first get on campus. I couldn't tell which way cutie swung, the way she was staring. Once they passed each other, we both looked back at the leather goddess. Weave tight, nice round ass with a model walk. She was high maintenance.

I sighed and turned back in the opposite direction to get one last glimpse of cutie walking the dog, but she was gone. I opened *Lisa's* back door and grabbed my jacket from the seat. As I began out across the lot, I notice Larry flagging me down and waving me in to the showroom. I cut across the lot and went inside to complete the paperwork. We rapped about this and that while he obtained my signatures in the necessary blocks and on the appropriate lines, then Larry grabbed hold of an overhead cabinet and pulled out my temporary tags. He gave me a congratulatory dap slap handshake and we left the showroom headed toward *Leslie*, my new boo. Yeah, I name my cars.

I pulled up next to *Lisa* in *Leslie* to empty out a few little things I still had with me: John Legend's new CD, *Evolver*, an old Three 6 Mafia CD, and an even old cup of coffee. People often heard my name and tried to tag me with a certain style, make me Muslim and whatnot. Just 'cause a brotha has an ethnic name don't mean nothing. My style is whatever's nice, whatever I'm feeling. Right now I'm feeling John Legend's joint! Last thing I grabbed was my parking decal for work. I said my goodbye to my late model and hopped in the new model. Leslie had plush wine leather seats and a wood- grained speaker Bose sound system. This felt good. Better than good, this felt right.

Even from a young age, I knew I had expensive taste. Never drank Kool aid, we could barely afford flavor aid. I was forced to wear thrift store clothes and those got further passed down to my younger brother, Kaisheem. I knew in junior high school that we were going to have to be real smart in order to have the things we wanted. I never hung out, never played sports or had any extracurricular fun. I was always about the books. Study, study, study. I was dumb as dirt. I thought all that time spent in the books would make me smarter! Hell, I barely got by.

The schools we went to didn't exactly have high standards. You got points for spelling your name out on every test. I must have gotten maybe two A's all through high school, the rest were c's. Man! I tell you wood shop was a pain, but I managed. I just couldn't focus.

My younger brother, Kaisheem, was the complete opposite. He played anything that moved, sports and women alike. He never studied and got damn near straight A's. He was always with me, so he hung out with an older crowd. I remember they used to tease him and say he was sleeping with half his teachers. Kaisheem never denied it. Kaisheem always got A's from his female teacher's. The lower grades came from his male teachers; go figure. Nevertheless, I was proud of him and encouraged him to keep up whatever it was he did. We had a plan.

As I drove up the beltway past my exit, I continued to reminisce. There was always something going on in my house growing up. Our daddy was a pimp. No really. We had ho's coming and going all the time, at all hours. Our mama was always strung out on whatever drug she could get a hold of. Always.

Kaisheem and I lived in a small room on the backside of the house. It was the only room that was out of sight. It was the only place for peace and quiet. Kaisheem is three years younger than me, but because of all the crap we went through growing up, you'd never know it. Like I said, I knew then that we had to be smart, get good grades and get the hell up outta that place.

We both knew. And that's what we both did. I struggled and barely graduated. Kaisheem graduated with honors. We went to whatever college would accept us and got whatever student loans we could get to pay for it. We worked whatever jobs we could get and did just about whatever else we needed to do for the rest of the money we needed. We lived however we needed to live to maintain and busted our ass through college to graduate.

I lucked out my junior year and interned with Hunter and Whitt, a legal firm that practiced sports entertainment law. I must

44

admit, I held it down in the accounting department the entire summer. I knew more than some of the permanent staff by the time my fall semester began. The powers that be were so impressed with my performance that they offered me a part-time job while I completed my senior year. Of course I took it.

Upon graduating, they made me full-time. It worked out perfectly. I had talked with Kaisheem once they made me permanent. Since I had worked with the firm a few years before Kaisheem graduated, I figured I could be able to get him a job there.

That is exactly how it worked out. Hunter and Whitt were more than ecstatic to hire Kaisheem. He was top of his class and coveted by a few other legal sports rep teams. So now this is us. Four to Seven years later, we were two black professional men working, playing bills and fucking a video ho on occasion. Nothing exceptional. No kids, no drama. Just JaRah and Kaisheem. Our friends see us and affectionately refer to us as "Dem Niggahs". We roll tight, always together. Well, we use to. You know the things that separate boys: women and money. Which one is it you ask? Both. I love my baby brother, but he is in love...with a gold digger.

I'm cruisin the beltway in my new BMW 750i, opening *Leslie* up, doing 120 easy, and my brother is up under some money digging, scheming woman. He should be here with me, taking this ride, windows down, cool air moving through the engine while I listen to T.I. and Rihanna sing our theme song, *"Just live your life....ayayayayaaa..."* But naw, that niggah is out spending his last dime to keep that gold digger's hair and nails done and keeps her in that expensive ass condo she rents. He keeps her clothes fresh and her belly full.

45

Kaisheem even had the nerve to ask me just last week if he could hold $50 because he had to take her out to the theater on Wednesday. Niggah are you serious? That's when we fell out.

I pleaded with my younger brother, "Kaisheem, for real, you need to let that bitch go."

"Don't start with me, man. Don't call her a bitch. I knew she was high maintenance when I met her," he said.

"Ok, so if you can't afford her, then you need to either let her know or let her go. Your relationship with her is becoming another bill for me. Kaisheem, man, I love you, not her. She can kick rocks. You, man, you're my little brother. This mess ain't no good for you. I'm telling you," I responded.

"I know what this is JaRah," he said. "You don't have anyone of your own to spoil. No shorty you can rock with, kick it with. That's on you. That's your decision. Now a days, they're all expensive. That's what you don't see."

"You know what Kaisheem? The answer is no. No 50, no 20, no 10, no 5, not even a quarter. No. No money for you and your ho."

"Whatever JaRah."

It's the same old discussion, all the damn time. I tell him I'm not giving him a hard time, then I turn around and give him a hard time. Eventually I feel bad for giving him a hard time and just give him the money. Maybe he's right.

Maybe I do need a shorty of my own to rock with. I got jump offs, but no shorty. I'm thinking about all this as I come up on Rockville. Damn, I'd been driving for like 40 minutes. I hadn't realized I'd gone up the beltway that far.

I got off on a random exit and got back on. Damn! I didn't even check the gas...WHEW! I'm good. I'm glad I thought of that before getting back on the beltway. I would have been standing at the pump twice in one day thinking, *Damn! Gas is expensive as a mug.*

Traffic up here is no surprise. Two things you always make sure of before you get on the beltway, piss and gas up. You never know if you'll be stuck in the far left lane miles from an exit. I continued reminiscing as I jumped back on 495 South. Thinking of who's got the best head. Thanks to a social networking website, Black World, I had been introduced to a couple of great jump offs. I thought to myself, *Who could I call to christen Leslie.*
Mental Rolodex:

- Tournesha. Damn! That girl could suck the skin off a peach. It had been a while since I hit up her page, left her an e-message. I miss the way she used to cradle my balls while she played with my head. I even let her stick her finger in my ass.
- Kelisha. Kelisha is a damn freak. She might make me crash my whip. Kelisha's an aggressive 4-foot-11 hood chick. She's small and light and bounces perfectly up and down on my pogo stick. Oh yes! Kelisha. The best thing about Kelisha is, she's so small I can see around her, but she's so damn wild with it. Naw, Kelisha would have me crashing the whip for real.
- Tiara. Mmmmmmmm mmmmmmmmmh! Tiara was something special. She was like the lady in the library who secretly used whips and chains. Tiara was a lawyer I met on

an account earlier this summer. Then I bumped into her on Black World. She has long legs, so the front seat is out.

Tiara must be about 5'11 and 160 lbs. Her measurements: 38 – 28 – 40. Discretion was her only request. Oh yes! Tiara. She does this thing with her fruit box that she called klinghon excercises or something. Anyway,

She can grip a brotha like a glove. She was open slidin' in and tight slidin' out. The sensation of the tight and not tight switchen up makes me climax hard. Damn Tiara! Damn, damn, damn! She could make a brotha feel bad about that. I mean, if I didn't concentrate, I could really get lost in the mix. Not cool. So...Who should it be?

Actually, I was feeling none of the above. I was getting older and I could tell my patience for needy jump offs was wearing thin. I needed someone to be settled with. Someone I could trust and love. I needed Sharlotte Swanson from Black World.

I had been chatting with this chick for the latter part of the summer and into the fall. I needed someone like her. Someone that had the potential to be the greatest love I'd ever known. True, I didn't know this chick from the next, but the conversation we had through e-messages and on the telephone had me thinking about where it was exactly that love came from. We all start out being strangers. Eventually we learn to trust and share. Somewhere along the way love develops.

Sharlotte wasn't a jump off. I hadn't even met her in person, but she had a special space in my mind. By now, I'm nearing my exit. I get over to the far right lane and get off the beltway. I pass the BMW dealership, pass Red Lobster and Strayer University. I make a right. I pass the Metro Station and make a left into my Condominium Complex. I press the button to open the gate and drive *Leslie* through and head toward my three level townhome.

Kaisheem's car is in my driveway. He has a key, but rarely comes over unannounced. We always call each before popping up. I open the garage and notice *Leslie* fits a little snug inside. I veer a little toward the right hand side of the garage, back up and straighten out.

Just then, the gold digger flings open the door leading from my garage to the lower level of my townhome. *What does this woman want and why is she at MY crib?* I asked.

She stood in a B-Boy stance with her arms folded, hips cocked to one side, rolled her eyes and neck.

"Why do you treat your brother like he ain't worth the time?" Olivia asked.

This woman done lost her mind. Then I asked, "I'm sorry, come again?"

I raised my left arm, tucked the right one towards myself as if to do the Heisman pose, pushed past her, and headed into MY house. I didn't look back, just heard her hit the wall in the garage behind me. I closed the door, hoping she was on her way to Kaisheem's car. She wasn't. She opened the door and stormed in behind me. Mumbling something about me being an uppity niggah.

Janine Coaxum

I called for my brother, "Kaisheem! Niggah, where you at?" I heard him on the second level, or maybe coming down the stairs on the third level.

He called back through the house, "Man! Where you put that Alizè from last weekend? Me and Olivia are headed out of town and I wanted to take that bottle with us, instead of buying a new one."

'Ole girl had walked past me and up the stairs to the second level and I was now headed in the same direction.

I called back to him as I approached the landing, "I put it in the cabinet above the fridge."

I heard him jump up on the counter. As I rounded the corner, I saw Kaisheem lookin' a hot mess. My man looked like straight garbage! I'm sayin'! We are clean brothas, always fresh and "GQ", but not Kaisheem today. Today, my little brother looked like a crack fiend.

Chapter Eight
Charlotte Swanson

"Everything isn't ever what it seems."

ll my single ladies, all my single ladies. All my single ladies, all my single ladies...uuh uh oh, oh oh. OH. oh oh! It's Friday and because I work 10 hours a day, I'm off on Fridays. So guess what, people? Friday is a good day. As I danced around my apartment singing Beyonce's new cut, I put away clothes, dusted, emptied the dishwasher and checked my inbox on Black World. I had checked *TonedTone1's* page to see if he was online; he was not. As I sang and floated from task to task, my mind raced. I thought about different projects at work, future appointments with hair clients and songs I would perform for upcoming gigs. I always had something on my mind.

Cocoa chewed on a bone as she watched what surely looked like an aimless dance from room to room, never accomplishing anything. I twirled over to the icebox to grab some water while singing...*If you liked it then you shoulda put a ring on it!* Then I guzzled my water.

My phone chimed. I hadn't received any harrassing phone calls for a month and a half. I hadn't thought about it all week, till now. For some reason, I just stood there. I didn't reach for my phone, wasn't anxious to see who was calling me. Then I did something I hadn't expected myself to do, I let it go to voicemail.

I walked over to my laptop and sat down. I placed the bottle of water out of reach on the kitchen counter and breakfast nook combo, because I'm clumsy. I wiped my hands on my pants and proceeded to check my inbox on Black World. Nothing. I decided to take Cocoa out for a stroll at the same time taking myself out for some fresh air. It was the beginning of October and it was definitely cooling off. I put on a jacket and hooked Cocoa up to her leash. My apartment complex consists of four buildings, each four floors high, that surround a six level parking deck. The remainder of the living community is made up of townhomes, three floors high with single or double car garages.

Townhomes that sell for $300,000 plus. The price disgusted me and made me miss the south even more. Cocoa and I strolled along in the mid evening sun. We walked down the side walk leading through the townhome side of the living community. We passed park benches and trees tied to the ground on both sides with what looked like 550 cord. We cruised the area, just chillin'. Then I heard a scream. It came from my right. I jumped and turned to see a white Range Rover speeding at me in reverse. I picked up Cocoa and shuffled onto the grass up close by one of the end units, just as the Range jumped the curb and left dirt on the sidewalk where I was just standing. The windows were tinted, so I couldn't see who was driving.

I looked back in the direction the Range came flying from and saw a single car garage door closing. I caught a glimpse of 30-day tags on a new BMW 750 that barely fit inside just before it closed completely. By now the Range Rover was put in drive and had completely made a mess of the grass on the opposite side of the street, where the sidewalk continued. It whipped around, wheels crunching in the wheel well as the driver turned the steering column as far as it would go to complete the turn, then sped off. I felt like I had interrupted something, like I had seen something I wasn't supposed to see. This was a nice, expensive community.

We had amenities. Hell, we had an amenity fee. A $500 amenity fee! Folks around here didn't pay all that money for this type of entertainment. Everything isn't ever what it seems.

Whoever was on the other side of that garage was probably really embarrassed. Whoever was in that white Range Rover was most likely very messed up.

I put Cocoa down. She looked at me as if to ask, *You sure it's safe, boss?* We turned and headed back to my building. Once inside my apartment, I went back to my computer. I checked my email and listened to J. Holiday talk about putting me to bed. I surfed back to Black World and checked my inbox. *You have an e-message from TonedTone1.* Well, it's about damned time. I know you remember when I first hit him up and got all excited once he responded. Let me catch you up.

We chatted online for about three months, on and off. We sent each other picture messages, even talked on the phone. We hadn't met yet, because we were both so busy. Either he was out of town or I was out of town. He had a late day or I had a late day. Our schedules really conflicted. Our conversations would spice up for a week or two, then die down when either of us was distracted by someone else (I'm guessing). We wouldn't talk for a week, and then we'd start right back up again, like we hadn't missed a beat.

Two busy bee's flirting amongst the flowers. That's what we were. I had learned a little more about him than what was on his page, but not much more.

He told me his name was JaRah Richmond and that he was from Mississippi and went to school at Fayetteville State University in North Carolina. He told me about his home life and that he and his younger brother did what they needed to do to get out and make a better life for themselves. He told me about his job and his promotion. He never talked about material things or money.

He never let on about his personal tastes or women. He didn't discuss his salary, where he lived or what kind of car he drove. I could appreciate that. It kept things simple. It kept me from having to discuss the same things.

Men were often intimidated by what I had going for myself. I owned a home in Georgia, drove a Mercedes CLS 500 and was making great money, despite the rags I wore and the apartment I lived in. That was a conversation I always hated having. I know now that it was because I was always having it with the wrong man. That's neither here nor there. JaRah Richmond. A breathe of fresh air, had blown into my apartment. I read his e-message.

Hey girl! I miss you. It's been crazy round my way. My brother is really trippin hard. I'm scared he might be on that stuff. N E way. I have time this evening to hang if you would do me the honor and accept my invitation to dinner. Woulda called, but I don't get great reception in my crib. You're guaranteed to receive this! Hit me back ASAP. -J

Ah! Dinner! I quickly hit the reply button. Just as I began typing, my cell phone chimed. I jumped up and ran to grab it. I thought JaRah must have gotten a signal now and was calling me. Instead it was an Unknown Caller with a 301 area code.

I answered, "Sharlotte Swanson."

"Fish Sticks and Grits, where were you today?"

"Who IS this? What do you want?" I questioned.

"Lollapalooza jam is on, we were supposed to be there, you stupid..."

END.

I was not about to let loony toons spoil my moment. I was getting ready to meet JaRah Richmond! Later for that other bull. My phone chimed again. This time, it was from a 202 area code. I let it go to voicemail.

I skipped back over to my laptop and finished typing my acceptance speech to JaRah. All the while, I'm annoyed I had even stopped to answer my phone.

SEND.

We arranged to meet at Maggiano's Little Italy Italian restaurant in Tyson's Corner at 8 p.m. sharp. I knew there was one closer in DC, but I was NOT about to try and find it in the dark. I told him what I would be wearing and how I'd have my hair. He did the same. We laughed because he said he'd be wearing clothes and that he was bald. So cute he was, still is. I digress. I cranked up the jam playing on my stereo, Bilaal and Boney James singing about me... *"It's getting better with time...it's getting better baby, so much better baby..."*

Chapter Nine
Dr. Tara Steele

"What's done in the dark will ALWAYS come to light"

I'm busy. So very busy. I'm always consumed with something. If it's not the practice, then it's my girls. If it's not the girls, then it's the evening classes I teach at the community college. If not the classes, then it's my mother or my sister. Some say I keep busy to avoid dealing with the reality of my situation. A reality we all have to swallow eventually. I'm not happy. I haven't been happy in a long time. I haven't talked about it because it's no one's fault but my own. I'm missing the kind of happiness only I can give myself. The happiness experienced when you've allowed yourself to love someone, fully and unconditionally.

I was married. He was an asshole. I wasn't happy. We got divorced and I felt better, but I still wasn't happy. The only time I can recall having the kind of happiness I miss right now, was in college. I found this inner peace and this self awareness when I met a particular man near the end of my freshman year. He was from Mississippi and I fell in love with his country boy accent. He was in a few of my elective classes and I noticed he was a ladies man. We spoke to each other in passing and even ate lunch together a couple of times. We talked about the Black Movement towards consciousness and discussed politics.

We never talked about "hooking up" because I had made it clear from day one. I wasn't a girl scout and he was cool with that. He knew he wasn't getting any of these cookies, not even on preorder with a promise to pay up front. It was my sophomore year at Georgia State Polytech and I ran into him at a local hole in the wall bar called Friendly's. I was with some dorm mates and he was with some older looking guys, maybe seniors or graduate students. We eye balled each other all night, him at the bar and me and my girls in a booth across the room. Finally, after thousands of stares and several drinks, he came over to our booth and spoke to me.

Richmond stood at the end of the table. I was seated on the outside of the booth. He leaned over toward me.

"Beauty, love, your first and middle name. Will you accept my last name as your last name?" he whispered in my ear.

"And what would that last name be?" I mouthed.

"Richmond," he said.

Richmond. I repeated his last name in my head, over and over. It rolled off his tongue something fierce. So soft and smooth. I could taste every letter, coated in Hennessy and coke. I'd known his last name, but just hearing him say it, reintroduced me to it. *Richmond.* He held out his hand to me and I accepted it. Standing to my feet, my head began to spin, much like my world upon his entrance. We walked past the bar, past his boys and over to a darkened corner. I closed my eyes, as he was standing behind me off to my left. I felt him graze my arm as he moved around to my right. He came around to my front and faced me. His eyes met mine again, as they had all night long. This time in close proximity. *Richmond.*

His skin was smooth, baby smooth, like butter. Like he skipped puberty, but was granted the endowments of a baritone voice and peach fuzz above his lip. *Richmond.*

He pressed his cheek against mine and it felt cold, smooth, soft and on fire all at once. *Richmond.*

He took my cup out of my hand and sat it down on a table nearby and pulled me close, never letting his cheek part from mine. Was I in love? I was wet. I could feel myself getting week. I was a virgin and had made a covenant with God to remain that way until marriage. I went off to college and started drinking. So far, not good....but tonight I was doing bad, worse than ever. I shuttered when I felt him. Down there. He was as hard as pool stick. I think I tried to pull away, but I can't remember exactly.

What I do remember is slapping the mess out of him and having him cuss me slam out while we stood in that dark corner. There, in a drunken stupor, Richmond laid into me about how I was a tease, I went to slap him again. He grabbed my hand mid air. My dorm mates were making their way over towards us. Richmond's buddies were still seated at the bar, laughing and high as kites on the fourth of July. I looked at him, he looked at me. We stood there, silently, in that dark corner, lights down low, music blaring, my wrist in his hand, both of us more turned on now then ever before.

*Lord Help!..I'm slippin'. I'm fallin'. I can't get up...*Tupac played in my head, over and over and over. He took me by my waste and whispered in my ear. I couldn't even tell you what he said because at the same time the wrist he held in his hand was being guided toward his third endowment, which I so selfishly forgot to mention earlier. There I was, standing so close to him. Richmond.

I held him in my hand. Yes! Held him in my hand. He had unzipped his pants and had set it in my hand like he had given me the key to the city. I felt like I was on the Price is Right and I had guessed the amount closest to the actual value. Oh, I was done. Stick a fork in me. It was a wrap. I was down for the count. It was so heavy in my hand. So thick and warm. Just then I ran my thumb over the width of it's beginning. He moaned and squeezed my shoulders. I was a virgin, but I was no stranger to this part of the male anatomy. I had learned many a trick to bypass or forgo intercourse and still keep my man happy. Let's just say, I got creative. It was slick. Ready-set-go seeped out into my hand, providing the lubrication needed to send him home. I stroked him. Right there, in Friendly's, over in that dark corner. Lights low, I stroked him. Music blaring, I stroked him.

More lubricant smoothed out my stroke and he began to rub my back. Then he laid his head on my shoulder as I
sped up. I felt his breath on my neck and my knees began to get weak right along with his. He squeezed me harder. I stroked harder. He squeezed me and I felt his drunken spit dribble out of his mouth and onto my collarbone before he sucked it back up and moaned. I stroked faster; I stroked harder. He was ready to explode, I felt him tensing up. Then he made the announcement, *"Oh baby, I'm gonna cum."* I kept stroking a good tight and steady stroke. My hand became creamy, his extra lubrication proved to be

more than enough to send him to his knees. He came hard, dropping to the floor and I went down with him.

I held him in my hand as I looked over at my dorm mates who stood by and watched the entire event. Mouths were open all around. His boys were now leaning on the bar, leaning hard. Eyes half open. Licking their lips and beginning to bulge and tell on themselves. My dorm mates were frozen. They were drunk, I was drunk, he was drunk. Hell, we were all drunk. I helped Richmond steady himself as he got up off the floor.

I immediately looked around for the bathroom so I could wash my hand. I spotted one on the opposite end of the bar, near the front entrance. I turned to go and Richmond said to me, almost out of breath, "*Will you stay with me?*" He looked so naked and vulnerable. I was confused. His voice was about two octaves too high for me not to consider this a punk move. I asked him to let me think on it while I washed my hands. He nodded and went for a chair while putting himself back together as best he could.

That night, I stayed with Richmond, and I was happy. We made love, even if we weren't *in* love. It was beautiful. Wonderful. Magical. All the positive words ending in –ful or –al, that's what it was. I was happy lying there in his arms. That was the beginning of my sophomore year. We did this on and off until graduation. We had never given ourselves titles. He saw other people, as did I, but I only gave cookies to him. I only shared the love that goes into making those cookies so delicious with him. He'd had several pregnancy scares with other women through all of which I stood by his side and supported him. I comforted and chastised him all in the same breath because I loved him. We went to the clinic together when he thought a girl had burned him, only to find he drank too much soda and had a urinary tract infection.

We went through it, he and I. Richmond. But I loved him and I was happy. Our relationship was so honest. It was so free from lies and deception. I hadn't had a relationship like that since Richmond. I now know, that's what would make me happy. We were free together, never judged each other. We talked about everything and nothing important all the time. I miss him. The day I met my ex-husband was a day I'll regret forever because I did some trifling mess.

It was my senior year, my last semester and I was pregnant. I was pregnant by Richmond. I was also seeing a guy I had met that fall before at an Opal Wednesday's restaurant where I waited tables. Richmond wasn't the marrying type. Even though what we had together, neither of us had with anyone else, Richmond was not going to settle down and marry me because I was pregnant. Enter Deception.

As soon as I missed my period, I gave in to my *guy friend* and had sex with him. You would have thought he won the lottery. I made it a superbowl like event. We had the pre-game show, the main event and even a postgame highlights reel. I needed to move fast though and quickly convinced him that I was the marrying type. That I wanted to have children, settle down and be a housewife and perform all the duties he believed a wife should perform. We had never been intimate before this because I was very satisfied by Richmond. I insisted that we not use protection, telling him that since I was a virgin, he needn't worry about any diseases. My *guy friend* went for it like a lamb to the wolves. A few days later he came back for more and that's when I played my hand. I told him that I felt guilty and that if he wanted any more cookies he'd have to marry me.

I worked him and worked him for weeks. Every week stressing out more than the week before, knowing that every week he held off on proposing was a week further away from me convincing him that the baby I would carry to full term would be his. Finally, after three weeks of talk and seduction and threats to leave him and end our relationship, my *guy friend*, John Steele, proposed to me. We married at the courthouse two days later. I never told Richmond I was pregnant, just said that this thing we had would end sooner or later. I told him our last night together. We had to grow up, move on. He would be graduating and going to work for a law firm in D.C. I would graduate and become a housewife and a mother. I've been unhappy in this particular way ever since.

My marriage to John Steel lasted for seven years, but was technically over from day one. I never loved him. I thought I would grow to love him because I liked him. We had a baby girl nine months after marrying. We named her Kayla. She looks exactly like me, thank goodness. She has a lot of Richmond's feature, but you wouldn't know it unless you knew Richmond. Five years later we had another baby girl, Shauna. Now Shauna looks just like her daddy, which is scary because it almost makes her and her sister look nothing alike. Almost. If it weren't for me, you wouldn't be able to see it.

John and I knew we needed to divorce when Kayla was six and Shauna had just turned 15 months. He rolled over in bed one morning, looked at me and said, "Who are you? Where is my wife?" With that he got out of bed, brushed his teeth, packed his toiletries in a suitcase with a few outfits, grabbed some suits he had on hangers, threw on some sweats and left the house. Before Shauna was born, when Kayla was three, I decided I had to go back to school. I couldn't just sit around the house and be a housewife like I'd promised I could. I'd been in school ever since, completing my Master's degree and starting on my Doctorate. That posed a wonderful way out for me, but our marriage crumbled quickly because of it.

I was never home. I didn't cook. I barely cleaned. It was all I could do to keep up with Kayla. I didn't have time for John. Sad thing was that it was fine with me. It was also fine with me when he left...and fine with me when he sent the divorce papers in the mail. Only thing that wasn't fine with me was the alimony he was requesting...talkin' 'bout he's become accustomed to this and accustomed to that! Bullcrap! It got ugly, real fast. He tried to say that he invested in my career, kept the household running and raised the kids while I went to school...Negro Please! I'm so glad we had a judge that saw right through him. All she had to do was ask him how the household bills were split up and paid. One stutter from that man and Her Honor rolled her eyes, banged the gavel and ruled in my favor. He got $300 a month from me before he remarried. That was it.

I remember leaving the courthouse. I left out first and was making my way to my car when John called out, "What's done in the dark will ALWAYS come to light." I had no idea what had caused his outburst. He had no idea how right he was.

Chapter Ten
Kaisheem Richmond

"I couldn't find myself because I had no idea how lost I was!"

When I was younger, my older brother did his best to take care of me. He did his best to make sure I ate, did my homework, had clean clothes and was generally in good health. I would watch him. I would watch his every move. I watched him sneak in Pops room when his ladies and Mama were nodding and take money. I would watch him when we went to the corner store for a pack of Kool's for our Uncle Q. I'd watch him talk to the clerk, telling him, *"Uncle Q sent us down here. Quit trippin'! You know we don't puff or dip! We just kids!"* I watched. I learned from him. Unfortunately, while I was learning from him how to live and survive, I was also learning how to pimp from our father and how to "feel good" from our ma.

Mixed messages. My life is so full of hypocrisies and mixed messages. I've always had this struggle inside. *Be smart, make good grade. Don't do drugs, sleep around or disrespect women. Have fun, drink this beer, bang this girl right here 'cause she wants it so bad. Hey...smoke weed everyday...*

Janine Coaxum

Sometimes I feel so screwed up I'm surprised I don't put my underwear around my neck and my necktie on my dick. I've always just barely made it. Not scholastically, 'cause that was always easy for me. Navigating the legal system, now there was a challenge. Being responsible for myself yet another challenge. There were so many times I ALMOST went to jail or caught a charge. JaRah just doesn't know. He'll never know as long as I'm still breathing.

Disappointment. I don't ever want JaRah to associate that word or any feelings that come from the word *disappointment* with me. I owe that man my life and more if I had it. That's my niggah for life, ride or die. He went before me in most everything in life. Always making sure the path was safe. At the same time he encouraged me to blaze my own trail, be my own man, and make my own mark in this world. I was always more book smart and street smart than him, but I never let him know it. I always knew the information before he gave it to me, but I would act surprised anyway. When he got accepted to Fayetteville State University, I was ecstatic.

I love my brother, but he struggled in school. I think he had an Attention Deficit Disorder, undiagnosed. He just couldn't focus, used to call himself dumb. When he got accepted to an Historically Black College and University, I almost pissed myself. JaRah was really book dumb. Nonetheless, I was proud of my big brother. He worked hard for everything we ever had. He deserved the opportunities he'd received.

In high school, I was all over the place. I played football, basketball, ran track, played soccer, was in the Drama Guild, on the Debate Team AND was Senior Class President. That was just what I did during the day. JaRah and I stayed in this little back

65

room at the house where Pops ran his tricks in and out while we were in elementary and middle school. Once JaRah got old enough to work, that's just what he did. He worked all kinds of jobs doin all types of work. He doesn't know I know, but when he was almost 17 he performed at strip parties for nasty old ladies. They must have paid well 'cause he did about four and we were set with a deposit and two months rent in a co-op. We stayed there for the remainder of our school days. I never worked, but contributed to the household just as well. I think JaRah knew where my money came from. Hell! I was the neighborhood weed man.

JaRah, being three years older than I, was always the responsible one. I told him before he went off to school that I could hold it down, pay the rent and utilities. JaRah insisted on paying everything up in full until I graduated in two years. That's what he did. I really didn't deserve a brother like JaRah. God paired us up the way he did because He knew how bad I was gonna screw up.

I'll begin with Georgia State Polytech. I went there on three partial scholarships that paid my tuition in full, Academic, Athletic and a Thespian Guild Scholarship. Don't laugh, that's money made legit! I ran the yard, ya heard! I've always been privy to the more mature crowd because JaRah took me everywhere. Now that I was out on my own, I had to develop my own swagger. I turned to the only other two males in my life to model myself after, Pops and Uncle Q. Now those two had swagger.

My pops was a natural born Pimp. I mean he could make a woman wanna touch herself, then get her interested in touchin' another chick and would collect the money from fellas wanting to watch. Pops was like the Don King of sex, always promoting. His brother, my Uncle Q, well, he was just a plain old sex machine.

Uncle Q went through as many cigarettes as he did women! If he wasn't mackin', he was sleepin'! It's a wonder my brother turned out the way he did. I often wonder what faults he inherited. I know which ones I got.

My days at Georgia Tech were filled with social, athletic and scholastic events, while my nights were all one big blur. That is 'till I met Ms. Tara Oleran. Tara! I had a ton of chicks runnin' after me my entire four years at Georgia Tech, but Tara was the only one whose name I remembered after hearing it the first time. We had intellectual conversations and she challenged me to be a better man sometimes. Other times, she was just cool, chill, somebody I could unwind with. I shared everything with Tara and eventually she shared everything with me.

I remember the first time we made love, *'cause that's what it was.* We met late one night in the neighborhood bar, Friendly's, a hole in the wall joint that had cheap liquor and loud music. I was out with my boys that night and I was soooo blown. I must have been high off weed, alcohol, and something else my boy Doug had given me to place on my tongue. I remember Tara sitting in a booth with her girls, cup in her hand, grooving to some cut that was blaring. I walked up to her and said something smooth. It must have been the right stuff 'cause she took my hand, got up and started grinding on me, getting me all hot. I hadn't seen this side of her before. Tara was DRUNK! Awe man! When I realized she was just as blown as I was, I went in for the kill. I led her over to a corner down past the bar. I remember moving in close, leaning into her neck and kissing on it. Suddenly, from out of nowhere, she hauled off and slapped me!

As soon as I got myself together I cussed her ass slam out. Then she raised her hand to swat me again. Her eyes were half closed and she was almost stumbling, trying to put force behind her swing. She was turning me on. Someone so in control of everything at all times was being caught off guard, CLASSIC! I caught her hand in mid-air, pulled my dick out with my other hand real slow and while I stared into her eyes, led Tara's hand to her destiny. I don't know what I was expecting her to do, but I know I didn't expect her to make me cum right there in that corner, in Friendly's. She did. Right there, lights low, music blaring.

That's exactly what she did. I came so hard, I got light headed and had to let the cold parquet wood floors support me for a moment. After everything spinning slowed down to a jiggle, Tara helped steady me to a chair. I felt played. Like I had made a bet in a poker game and she read my face, called my bluff. I didn't want her to ever leave me. She turned to walk away and something in me panicked. There, in that hole in the wall bar, lights low, music blaring, I wanted to marry Tara Oleran. I wanted this woman, the only woman to ever bring me to my knees, match me in wit and passion. I wanted her to be mine and no one else's. I asked her to stay with me that night. She did and for many nights to come after that.

I was in love. Tara had me lost. I couldn't find myself because I had no idea how lost I was! Tara was my world, aside from my brother. Towards the end of my junior year, Ma and Pops got busted in a raid and went to prison for a 10-year stint each. Neither JaRah nor I took it hard; it was a long time coming. We actually hoped it would help dry Ma out, but we knew better. After you've been druggin' for so long, to stop without any medical assistance is a heart attack or stroke waiting to happen.

Tara and I lay in each other's arms on a lazy afternoon. We were stretched out the full length of my futon, entangled in each other like a pretzel and watching our favorite Spike Lee Joint *She Hate Me* when there was an abrupt knock at the door. I untangled myself from her, got up from my futon and opened the door. On the other side of the frame stood my Dorm Resident Assistant, Andre.

"Sup?" I started.

"Kaisheem, we just got a fax from the Mississippi State Correctional Facility where your Mother is."

Andre handed me a fax.

I read it out loud...*Mr. Kaisheem Richmond:*

The Mississippi State Bureau of Corrections regrets to inform you that your mother, Nadine Richmond, passed away yesterday morning at 0534 a.m. from a massive heart attack.

"I knew it," I said in a low voice.

Tara put the DVD on pause and was standing behind me. I stepped back from the door. Andre gave me his condolences while I closed the door slowly. JaRah.

I needed to call my brother. My heart wanted to scream. I wanted to cry, but I couldn't find any tears. We knew this would happen eventually. It was either this or a drug overdose. Our mother lived hard, always keeping a high that kept her numb, oblivious to the world she lived in.

Simply put, our mother stayed high and we knew that when she came down, the weight of the world would come crashing down on her and crush her heart. Her soul would be let loose from her body and she would be free. She need only come down off that permanent high. I sat back down on the futon. Tara sat down next to me. I stared deep into the wall in front of me. I didn't really focus on any one thing in particular, I just stared. Then I heard Tara calling my name.

"Kaisheem. Kaisheem, do you want me to ring your brother? Where is your phone? Kaisheem..."

I turned to look at her and when my eyes met hers, it fell. It finally fell. That tear that was stuck in my eye since I first saw my ma get high when I was 4 years old. The tear that teased and taunted me stung like dirt in my eye, making my eye water constantly, but never enough for any relief.

That one single tear fell. It was thick and heavy and had years of pain in it. It rolled so slow down my face I thought It might evaporate before making it to my chin. It didn't. That big thick heavy tear rolled on for what seemed like forever, tickling and aching me. It reached my chin and Tara kissed it, she wouldn't let it hit the ground. I knew then, I was going to find a way to keep her in my life forever.

The rest of that week, let alone the rest of that day, was a blur. I drank and smoked the night away, went numb in memory of my ma. The following school year, I decided to do one of the dumbest things ever. I was going to get Tara pregnant on purpose. I figured if she were pregnant, we'd have to get married. I still had jump offs, but I made sure to slow my pace on that scene. I cut a bunch of chickens loose. I tried all fall semester, bustin' loose left and right, all up in her. No such luck. No *"Kaisheem, we need to talk."* What was I doin' wrong? I know my soldiers were marching because I'd had to tell Tara about two scares and one confirmation two semesters ago. Damn! I couldn't lose her.

I'd considered just coming right out with a proposal, but we weren't even dating! How was I going to ask this woman who I loved with all my heart to marry me and have her actually take me seriously? As smart as I was, when it came to Tara Oleron, I was the village idiot. Spring Semester, we didn't hang as tight. Tara assured me it was because of her comprehensive exams. I had to remember, I was smarter than a lot of my peers, and academics came easy to me. I didn't know how to study? I could just review information and have it from then on.

I continued to try. Every chance I got, which wasn't that many, I was sending my soldiers off to war. A war for Tara's heart, forever. None made it back home to me. That left me sad. Sort of empty inside. This was a new and uncomfortable feeling for me. I played it off with all my peers, my boys, the couple of jump offs still hangin' around and more importantly, I played it off with Tara. The last time I held her in my arms was late April, just after spring break. It felt like goodbye. We lay there in each other's arms, talking. My soldiers marching, hopefully.

"Kaisheem, you know I've been seeing that guy John. Right?"

"Right. Him. What about him? He do something to you?"

"No, I just...I think he might be serious."

"Serious how?"

"Serious, like marriage."

I rolled onto my side to look her in the eye for this next question.

I asked her, "Do you love him?"

She giggled and squirmed like she was uncomfortable, but there wasn't anything funny, clearly. Either she was uncomfortable because she did love him and didn't know how to tell me or because she was about to lie to me.

She said, "What do you mean, do I love him? If he wants to marry me and I DON'T love him, I'll just learn to love him."

"Has he proposed to you or something? Why are you bringing this up, here, NOW?" I was beginning to show emotion. I shouldn't have.

"Are you catching feelings or something? No not you! Not Kaisheem, the P.I.M.P. Machine," she said hurting me more than I ever thought it would. I think she could see the pain in my face, but she continued on, like this was something she needed to say. Like this was burning a hole in her soul.

"Kaisheem, you should just be concerned about yourself. Don't worry about me. We can't all *play* for the rest of our lives. I know that what we have is special and I hold it dear to me, but you're never going to be serious enough with yourself to settle down and marry any woman. You'll never be content with just one person."

That was the last thing she said to me. She got up, got dressed and left. She left me. She left my room, left my world. She was gone. Just like that. Three years of laughter, high fives, moans and strokes of gold, gone. Over. Tara was gone.

I looked for her at graduation in May and didn't see her in the line-up. I asked around for her and one of her dorm mates said she had gotten married and wasn't going to walk because she was pregnant. Pregnant? PREGNANT!

My heart raced. It beat so fast, I thought I might be sick. My world spun. It spun out of control. I almost passed out standing, waiting to walk across that stage. As I approached the steps of the stage, all I could think of was my many soldiers that I had sent off to war. Had they completed their mission? If Tara really was pregnant and that's why she didn't walk, could it be my child? I believed the part about her being married because of our last talk. But PREGNANT? I hoped that she was. I wanted desperately to find her. I wanted to...

"Kaisheem Richmond. Kaisheem Richmond." They were calling my name and I didn't even realize it. It took a couple of nudges from those behind me to get me going. I walked across the stage, but I wanted to run. Run out into the streets and call her name. I wanted to find her.

I had a job lined up at the firm my brother was bustin' his ass at...I wasn't looking forward to that, but I was grateful all the same. I packed up everything I owned and loaded it in my Explorer. All the while, I thought of her. She was somewhere, pregnant with a small, round belly barely showing. A life, created by us. I think. I hope. My college years proved to be maturing against my will.

What happened between Tara and me caused me to grow inside. It also caused me to harden. I started to believe she was right. She was right about me not being able to settle down with just one woman. Especially since the only woman I wanted to settle down with was her. How ironic that she would be right, only because of events in my life SHE set in motion.

Fast forward 10 years. Here I am working in Washington, D.C., living in Maryland, and enjoying the life. I'm loving the night scene and still playin', but not as many different hands. I'm currently seeing this woman, Olivia. She's high class and high maintenance, but she's fun, which is exactly what I want in my life right now. So, maybe she's not Mrs. Right, but she's Mrs. Right

Now. Olivia actually reminds me of the only two women I ever loved. She's smart like Tara and gets high on the regular like my Ma.

Chapter Eleven
Tara and Sharlotte

"I could be Mrs. Richmond"

I had a date. I was finally going to meet JaRah. No more picture messages. No more late night steamy conversations to set my dreams and desires in motion. I was going to see the real thing. Meet the man behind the curtain. I was excited! I had to call up Tara. I had told her about JaRah on several other occasions. Made her privy to information he had given me. She was happy for me and concerned at the same time. Seeing as I had been through so many "Internet dates" that went horribly wrong, she was warranted in her caution.

First there was the alcoholic. He was an attractive, slightly younger man. Andrew. He had been in the Navy for four years. He did his tour and decided not to re-enlist for *The Man*. Andrew was adamant about not fighting in a war he didn't support. I understood. Andrew and I talked for about a month via e-messages before we decided to meet in person. We made a date to go to the movies. Andrew then told me he had lost his license because of a DUI earlier in the year. This didn't alarm me because we all make mistakes. I can't count the number of times I barely made it home.

I was sitting at stop signs waiting for them to turn green. I didn't judge him, I just rolled with it.

I arranged to pick him up from his residence, which turned out to be his mother's.

Again. I didn't judge him. I just rolled with it.

I know. The list. I know, but like I also stated, the pickins were slim, so I had to make do.

Andrew was sweet, not very articulate, not very smart and sweet all the same. I arrived at his address and rang the bell. He came to the door almost immediately as if he had been standing on the other side of the door waiting for me. He flung open the door and instantly I heard an older woman fussing.

"Yeah. Alright, Ma. I'm gone!"

He closed the door, being sure to lock it from the inside first. We greeted each other with a hug and walked to my car.

"Oh you rollin' big, Ma," he said commenting on my Mercedes CLS 500.

"Well, you know, I do alright."

"That's what's up!" he exclaimed.

I pressed the button to unlock all doors. We got in and were off to the Magic Johnson theater at Largo Town Center. During the drive there, we made small talk, which was difficult because he really wasn't very articulate at all. I didn't judge him, I just rolled with it.

I smelled a hint of alcohol in the air when he talked. It was 3:30 in the afternoon. My concerns about "just rolling with it" grew.

Once we got to the theater, I parked and we went inside. Andrew got to the door first, extending his left arm, while holding his jacket closed with his right. I expected him to open and hold the door for me. He didn't. Andrew shot through the first set of doors and was working on the second set as I reached for the closing first set of doors. I no longer felt like rolling, but I was already out with him.

Once we got to the ticket counter, Andrew stood at the window, off to the side and waited for me to select the movie.

I told the attendant, "One for Step Brothers". Andrew looked at me. I looked at him, daring him to complain.

The attendant quoted me the price and waited for me to hand her payment. I looked at Andrew.

"Aren't you going to get a ticket?" I asked him.

"Look Ma, I thought the matinee would be less. I ain't got that," he replied. Oh my dear sweet baby Jesus. I just looked at him, judgingly.

"So what do you got?" I asked him.

"I have five dollars. You got the rest?"

"No. I don't. So I guess we're not going to the movies."

"My bad, Ma. I just didn't leave the house with much cash and my moms has my card. Tell you what. My man has the bootlegs for a couple of new movies that are out. Let me call him and see if we can scoop one."

We moved away from the attendant and headed out of the theater. I was so disgusted. He made a phone call as we walked to my car. He hung up and asked me if I felt like swingin by his boy's house to pick up a bootleg. At this point, I didn't think it could get much worse, so I obliged. Hell, I had gotten cute and left the house. I was gonna see somebody's something before going back home. We got in my car. As I was putting on my seatbelt, Andrew reached inside his coat pocket and pulled out a fifth of some no name dark liquor, cracked the top and took a swig. This was NOT happening.

I looked at him. He screwed the cap back on and tucked the bottle back inside his jacket. I was still looking at him. He paid me no attention. I asked him to put his seat belt on as I started the engine. He did so. As he gave me directions, everything in me screamed, *TAKE THIS NIGGAH BACK TO HIS MAMA!* Did I? You guessed it. Nope. I followed directions.

We picked up the movie from his boy, a movie I had already seen. I didn't make mention of this. I just wanted to get him home. Andrew took swigs. I followed directions.

We arrived at his house, correction, his MAMA's house and I parked. I didn't get out. Andrew didn't notice. He struggled with the seatbelt. I could tell he was both drunk and not used to operating the contraption. It was now 5:23 in the evening.

He got out and staggered toward the steps to his door. I sat in my car. Andrew turn toward the parking space.

"You not coming in?" he asked.

I rolled down the passenger window and yelled,

"No, you enjoy. I'll holla!"

With that I put it in reverse and left. Didn't see or hear from Andrew again.

Then there was Crazy Chris. Ugh! Chris was so insane. I mean clinically delusional. I should have known better from the beginning with this dude. Again, we met on Black World. He commented on a picture of mine.

"Isn't she lovely? Look at my future wife to be. Isn't she lovely!" he said.

Okay, first off, I was flattered. I had no idea the man was serious. We chatted back and forth through e messages for about two weeks before he insisted on seeing his *bride to be.*

Again, I was flattered. I didn't think he was serious. I was stupid.

He whined and begged about meeting up. So I finally gave in and obliged him. I was going out of town and told him I would meet him at a Metro Station near the beltway exit between our locations. I pulled up first and waited. I had given him my phone number so that we could coordinate our travel. He called me asking if I had arrived. I told him I had and that I was waiting near an out of service Metro Bus. Chris assured me he was on his way and was fighting traffic. I told him to take his time. Twelve minutes later his car pulled up next to mine. Chris got out and approached me, open arms and a big smile on his face.

"I missed you! Where have you been all my life?" he asked.

I was completely thrown off. Not knowing what to say or how to react, I gave Chris a hug. I let go way before he did and had to endure the remainder of his portion.

"So when are you coming back?"

"I should be back by the end of the weekend."

"Ok, you're not answering my question. So when should I expect you?"

"Maybe I'm not answering your question because that's none of your concern."

Chris looked confused and frankly so I did it.
Now, I know you're getting the abridged version, but trust me, I've left nothing out. Chris's behavior was just as inappropriate and unwarranted as I'm presenting it to you. I stood there, looking at him. He was tall, medium built, wore fake glasses, had a bald head and was clean cut. I wasn't interested. Not in the least.

I began to talk, "Chris, it was really nice meeting..."

79

"Look. When you get a chance, tell my future mother-in- law I said, *Thank You* for creating you."

"Excuse me. You cut me off. You know what, I thought you were very flattering in the beginning, but now you're just making me uncomfortable."

Chris looked even more confused and then a wave of anger covered his face. Thanks for the cue, Lord! I told him goodbye and got in my car. Man! I'm so dumb.

My phone chimed as I headed out the Metro Parking lot.

It was Chris.

I answered, "Yes, sir."

"You didn't have to leave like that. You could have let me finish talking."

"I apologize, but it doesn't seem like we're on the same sheet of music..."

He cut me off, chiming in with, "Well, maybe we just need to talk more. I'll call you later on this evening once you get where you're going. Where are you going?" Chris didn't get it and that worried me. I said to him as calmly as I possibly could, "Chris, I'm not interested in getting to know you any further. There is no need to call me anymore."

"Alright then. Cool. Just know that you're selfish and that everything can't always be on your terms. You're spoiled too, you know that! I don't need this."

END.

Chris hung up on me. I immediately changed his name in my phone to DNA (Do Not Answer) Crazy Chris.

There are so many more stories. So many DNAs. So many more encounters with "the third kind". There was the weed head, the married man, the police detective, the firefighter, my next door neighbor...the encounters alone are a completely different story. Just know that I was taking a chance with JaRah, going out on yet another limb. Each encounter had me climbing higher into my tree for safety. Every time I went out on a limb, the risk was greater, because I was farther from the ground. You can just about imagine how high up I was by now. If I fell this time, it just might have been my death.

I was willing though...a willing participant in this mating game. I was a closed book not bound by anything but string made with love. If you had no love for me, that string would cut you as you tried to unbind me. At this moment, I'd hoped JaRah had it in him to love me. Unbind me, so that I could be read in truth.

My phone conversation with Tara continued.

"So when are ya'll meeting? What are ya'll going to get into?"

"We're meeting at Maggiano's at 8 p.m. sharp. We're just going to have dinner, sit and talk. You know, nothing major."

"Dinner huh? Who's for dessert?"

We giggled like school girls.

"I'm saving the cookies for dessert for another day," I replied.

"Yeah right! Don't forget who you're talkin to. I know good and well you'll give him the cookies if he breathes on you and his breath is fresh!" I laughed hard. She was so right. I recomposed myself.

"Well, you ain't my girl for nothing, but for real, I am going to try my best to hold out. I just hope he's not a bust. If he's good, I could be Mrs. Richmond." The sound of *Mrs. Richmond* brought an awkward silence.

"Hello? T! Did I lose you?"

"I'm here...Mrs. Richmond? What's his name again?"

"JaRah Richmond. I never told his full name. Did I?"

"No..... no you didn't."

Tara said that with conviction. A conviction that had me feeling guilty, like I had left something terribly important out of our previous conversations. I was expecting further interrogation from her, but it ended.

Tara was silent. She had no more questions. I could barely hear her breathing. I asked, "Girl! What's going on? Is there something wrong? Do you know him? If you know something, you need to tell me!" Silence.

"T!"

"No Sharlotte, I don't know him. I just have a lot going on. I'm a little distracted right now. That's all."

I didn't believe her. I knew when Tara was lying to cover up her thoughts and feelings. She was always so obvious.

Tara continued to lie to me, "You get sexy and have a good time tonight. I wanna hear about it when you get home so call me first thing in the morning."

I laughed a little, as I had caught her slick reference to my location NOT being home till the morning. My reply was soft and consoling, as I knew something was wrong with Tara. We got off the phone and I proceeded to get ready for my date with JaRah.

I went into my living room and cranked up the mix CD I had been playing on repeat all day. Jasmine Sullivan was telling me about that oh so familiar plight of heart, singing *Boy I need you bad as a heartbeat, bad like the food I eat, bad as the air I breath.* Cocoa was doin' what Cocoa does best, chewing on a bone. I sang along with Jasmine as I went into the bathroom to start my shower. I let the water get hot and peered at myself in the mirror as I peeled off my clothes.

I was beautiful. Tall, lean with meat in all the right places. No children yet, but my hips were ready. My breasts were full, round and supple. I worked hard to keep myself looking good. It was all to please me. If you keep yourself pleased, all others will follow suit. Anyone not willing to get with the program should be shown the door. Steam rose from behind the shower curtain and my image in the mirror became fogged. I pulled the curtain to the side and stepped in.

Ahhhhh. That first drop of hot water was a shock, but the rest that came after were all welcomed hugs against my skin. I turned in a circle to wet myself all over. I grabbed my washcloth to lather up with organic soap free body wash. I did that three times to make sure I hit the hot spots. I paid homage to the cookie jar. Rinsed. Repeated. I could easily take a 30 minute shower. I realized that I hadn't paid attention to the time. I shut off the water, threw the curtain back and peered through water dripping in my eyes for the clock.

No!! 6:45. Tyson's Corner was at least 30 minutes away, 20 if traffic was good. I dried off and zoomed through my closet. *Should I wear a dress? Easy access...nope, I don't need any help in that department. Jeans? No, not dressy enough. Slacks? No! Sharlotte, you're not going to work! Damn!* I settled on a floor length black pencil skirt with a nice slit in the side that ended at my knee.

I complimented it with a black short sleeve sweater that had a black and white pinstriped design on the breast with ruffles around the arms and neck. 7:15. I needed to go, so I threw my hair up in a loose ponytail. I grabbed a pair of black pumps that were already by the door. Sprayed some perfume in the air and walked through it. Put Cocoa up in her kennel and gave her a treat, made sure everything was off, grabbed my coat, my purse and shot out the door.

On the way to my car, my cell phone chimed. I dug through my purse.

I answered, "Hey, girl!" Silence.

"T? You there?" Bad reception, I had no bars.
The call ended.

I hit my last called button and scrolled down the list two names to her number. Just as I was about to dial Tara again, her name popped up. I answered.

"Hey, girl!"

"Are you gone yet?" Tara asked.

"I'm getting in my car right now. Why? What's up?"

"Nothing. Things have calmed down over here and I wanted to talk to you some more before you went out. I was just wondering how much this guy actually knows about you. You be careful ok," she said.

"I will."

"What DOES he know about you? I mean, what have you told him?" she asked.

"Well, I told him the usual stuff. What I do for a living, where I'm from, family demographics, likes and dislikes..."

"Did you tell him about us?" she asked.

84

"Well, I told him about you being my best friend and that the move hasn't slowed our conversations any. Why?"

"Just wondering," Tara said.

I turned onto the ramp and got on the beltway. Our strained conversation continued, "Tara, you're not being honest about something. What is it?"

"What do you mean? There's nothing for me to be honest or dishonest about!"

I had offended her, which meant I had hit a sore spot, the truth. I love my Girl, dearly, but she wasn't honest with me about a lot of things. I knew this, but never let on about it. Tara continued, "I can't be concerned for you? I mean you do have a stalker, in case you've forgotten about that. I don't want you putting my business out there and putting me at risk too!"

"Oh! So that's what I'm doing huh! Well SMACK me! My bad! I won't tell anybody about you from now on. Wouldn't want somebody to come looking for your ass across 1 state lines! No sir-e-bob! Wouldn't want that at all!"

I was getting annoyed with this conversation and the direction Tara was trying to take it in.

"Sharlotte, that ain't what I mean and you know it. I'm just saying, watch what you tell people. You never know who knows who. Six degrees of separation Sharlotte. That's all."

I merged onto 495 towards Tyson's Corner. 7:40.

"OK. I hear you."

Tara let out a sigh. A heavy sigh. Then she closed the conversation, "I don't want you to be irritated. That's not what I called to do. I'm just worried. We don't know who it is calling you. It could be anyone. Just don't be so trusting. OK?"

I rolled down the driver's side window to create enough noise that would make the conversation unbearable to continue and said, "OK. I hear you."

"What is that noise? Sharlotte, did you let down the window? OK, I know what that means; we'll get off the phone."

"I love you. Bye, girl!" I said.

"Bye, girl. Love you too!"

Tara---A.K.A. Ms. Devil's Advocate---A.K.A. Ms. Buzz Kill. Nonetheless, I love her to death, but she ain't foolin' me. There was something in that conversation that I wasn't getting. Something I was missing, but I couldn't put my finger on it. I tried to play the conversation over in my mind from the beginning. Nothing stood out, but the silence. Silence when I told her JaRah's last name. My mind raced as I hit my exit off of 495. It was 7:53. I was going to be on time, just barely. I needed more time to get my mind right. Too many thoughts, all racing for first place in my think tank. I had to take a minute and prepare myself for a slower, deeper conversation with JaRah. I had to take deep cleansing breaths.

I pulled into the Galleria II and drove around looking for a parking space. White lights. Someone up ahead was backing out, so I waited. As soon as they cleared the space another car zoomed from another isle over and grabbed the spot. *Sonofabitch!* People up north are so rude! I let off the brake and rolled by, staring at the BMW 750 with 30-day tags that had snatched my spot. *I know you saw me waiting, but that's ok. Karma is a bitch.* I sped up and went down about five isles over, found a spot and parked. My cell chimed.

It was JaRah. I answered, "Hey! Where are you?"

"I'm here, about to get us a table. What's your preference, smoking or non?"

"Non. Please."

"Where are you?" he asked.

"I just parked, I'm on my way in now." In the sexiest and cheesiest phone sex voice I could muster, I asked, "What are you wearing?" JaRah let out a hearty laugh that was now muffled by the background noise of people eating and conversing. "Girl, get in here so I can show you! You'll know me when you see me. I'll be the one excited to see you and wearing a hard on!" I laughed. I hoped so.

"Ok, I'm coming, bye!" We both giggled at that one.

"Ok, bye and hurry!" JaRah hung up.

I checked my lip-gloss in my visor mirror and adjusted a few strands of hair that had been set astray when I let my window down. I collected my purse, my phone and my keys, got out and headed toward the restaurant. I pressed the button to lock my doors several times just to be sure.

I had several looks and stares that reaffirmed I was fly. I walked slowly and careful through the parking lot, crossed the street and stepped up onto the curb. There was a line coming out of the double doors of the Galleria for Maggiano's. I'd hoped JaRah wasn't standing in this line. I looked through the line for his bald head and broad shoulders. He wasn't in it. I entered through a second set of doors, went around several people, saying excuse me and pardon me all the way as I entered the restaurant.

The smells of olive oil, pasta's, garlic and tomatoes were welcomed into my nostrils. I looked at the tables. People eating, smiling, sipping wines and slurping noodles. Then I saw him. He was over in a corner booth toward the back right of the restaurant. His face glowed in the dim light. He was gorgeous. He slid out of the booth and moved through the crowd toward me.

He was tall, taller than my 5-foot-8 frame. His shoulders were strong and his jaw line square. Much more handsome than any picture could ever do him justice. I melted. My heart beat hard in my chest. I moved toward him and met him halfway. We stopped short of each other by about three feet. We looked, stared at each other. Me at his eyes. Him at mine. His mouth was open in a smile that displayed slick shiny pearly whites, lots of them! He closed his mouth, held out his hand.

"Sharlotte, may I?" He motioned to seat me at the booth. I nodded to oblige him and as I passed him, we touched. Our bodies touched. My shoulder brushed his chest. His belt buckle grazed my hip. My thigh caressed the part of him that let me know he was happy to see me. I turned to slide in the booth and his face came to meet mine. In surprise I turned my head to face him.

As my butt plopped down on the seat, his lips met mine. Oh! My! So soft! So unbelievably soft. Minty fresh like real mint leaves. Sweet like peach juice. So soft and so sweet. We were in a lip lock for what felt like minutes. Normally the position I was in, with him standing and me sitting, would have felt awkward, but this...his just flowed...felt natural...felt good.

We released each other. He stood erect. I motioned for him to have a seat on the other side of the booth. He looked down and did so, quickly. I smiled a smile so big, I could feel my cheeks cramping up. We looked into each other's eyes and just smiled. There was a lot of smiling going down. Neither of us broke the stare, not even when the waiter came to take our drink orders.

Janine Coaxum

When asked what we would like to drink, we said in unison, "Water."

Chapter Twelve
JaRah and Kaisheem

"You're not him and you'll never be him"

"I'm tired of arguing with you about Olivia!"

"Then leave her the hell alone! Ditch her ass!"

"No! I don't see you suckin' me off how I like it!"

"Man please! If that's all she's good for, you've got plenty more heads where she came from. Just let her go. Kaisheem, please. This chick is taking you to a place you might not come back from."

"I'm tired of listening to your same 'ole broken record, JaRah. Olivia is my girl. We ride together, Bonnie and Clyde style. She's not going anywhere."

"Then the answer is no. No, Kaisheem. No money for this weekend. No you can't take my car. No you can't borrow my linen suit and no you can't use my timeshare. NO!"

"You know what, JaRah? You're NOT my father. You're not him, and you'll never be him! Damn, man! What happened to us, JaRah? When did it get like this?"

"When you lost yourself in a woman who was no good for you!"

When JaRah said that, I thought back to Tara. Forget about Olivia, she was just a girl who was the best I'd found so far in covering up my pain. Pain I'd been living with since graduation, 10 years of pain, wondering if I had a child out there. A woman out there who I loved and a child who I wished I could love. A family. A family outside of JaRah. I was losing it and I knew it, but I didn't care. I was just barely making it at work. I turned in paperwork hours before deadlines, missed meetings, and brushed off company parties. Lately I spent all of my nights and a good deal of my days getting high with Olivia. When she wasn't at a shoot or on location, we were living it up. Drinking, smoking, and screwing.

Olivia was a model/actress. She'd done some print work for La Rue Cosmetics and a couple of Fit Tight Jeans ads. Now she was pursuing films. She hadn't gotten anything big, just a couple of shots as an extra in the background. Recently, she grabbed a part in an action/adventure film featuring that guy from the movie *Baby Boy*. I listened when she talked, but I didn't care. As long as she supplied the weed and the head, I was good.

Olivia is not anyone I would ever split with family over, but for some reason, I defend her to JaRah. All my life, I've listened to him. I felt that I owed him that. We're adults now, but I sometimes feel like he doesn't realize that. So I buck against him. I don't listen to what he has to say. I rebel. Damn! It sounds like we're kids again, I know. That's my whole problem. I often think of Tara and what she said to me that night. I wonder if she was right. I hold on to that night and replay it in my mind, over and over.

I joined JaRah in the conversation he'd been having with himself while my mind wandered.

"Kaisheem. Man, I'm not trying to tell you how to live your life. I'm not! I just don't want to see you turn out like Ma." At that moment something snapped.

Janine Coaxum

I got this overwhelming sensation to wanna get high. Be numb. Numb like I felt the day our mother died in prison. Numb like she had been all of our lives. I gave JaRah a look that made his face change. He started toward me, arms open.

"Man I'm sorry. I didn't mean to hurt you."
I backed away. In that moment I knew. My brother had known about my drug use. He'd known all these years and had never said a word. I turned to leave his townhome. He reached for me and grabbed my arm. I jerked away and threw up my fist. I was angry.

JaRah. My brother. My protector. My handicap.
I had to get away. Clear my head. I shot down the stairs toward his garage. His footsteps in sync with mine, only inches away.

"Kaisheem? Please, man wait!"

"What, JaRah?"

"Look, just call me later. Okay? I love you, man."

"Yeah. I love you too."
I opened the garage door and headed towards my white Range Rover. It was a mess. It was dirty from not having been detailed for weeks. Yet another tell tale sign of my disdain for things in life. I got in and slammed the door. My world started to spin. I started the engine and looked up at JaRah as he stood in the doorway. I threw it in reverse and slammed on the gas. I hadn't thought about which way I had cut my wheels when I pulled up in JaRah's driveway and skirted out backwards at an angle. My Range bounced as I hit the curb. My tires slipped in grass until they hit the sidewalk. I looked to my left and right, only to see a woman holding a small dog looking back at me with fear in her eyes. I knew she couldn't see through my limo tint, so I ignored her. Put the Range in drive, cut the wheel as hard as I could and sped off. I

wouldn't call JaRah tonight. Tonight, I was going to get high one last time. High on something good. High on Olivia.

***

Damn it. Damn it. Damn it. Why did I have to open my big mouth? Kaisheem had just left and I knew he was going to do something stupid. He was already on thin ice at the firm. They had not been pleased with his performance over the past year and were threatening to lay him off. He had notices from bill collectors and just last week we were down at the bank paying out big money because he was three months behind on his mortgage.

Damn! What have I done? Have I made him irresponsible? Is all of this My fault? I realized that in loving him I had deceived him. I led him to believe life was something it wasn't. I let the garage door down just as he hit the curb. Damn Kaisheem. I was so lost. Kaisheem is the only family I've got. True, our pops is still kickin' it in state prison with only a couple more months in his sentence and Uncle Q will be there waiting at the gate upon his release, but it has ALWAYS been me and Kaisheem. Dem niggahs.

As the garage door closed, I headed upstairs to my laptop. I got online and checked my company email. No new business. I checked several other emails, including my inbox on Black World.

Sharlotte. I smiled when I thought of my online buddy. She was the comedic relief for most of my days. We'd sent each other e-messages back and forth, exchanged pictures and even telephone numbers. Our phone conversations were unlike any I had with other females. Sharlotte was real. She was very open and knew a little bit about everything. Smart and a smart ass. I loved talking to her. I admit.

93

Janine Coaxum

I could have done a better job at getting to know her, but my jump offs were all needy. I had myself spread thin at times. No matter how busy I got, with work or play, every time I went back to her it was like I never left. Sharlotte never questioned me or fussed me out for not having emailed or called her. She treated me like I was a grown ass man and I treated her like she was a grown ass woman.

She looked thick in all of her pictures. She had so many different hairstyles; I couldn't tell exactly what she looked like. Her face was beautiful and so was her spirit. That was good enough for me, till now. In this moment, I wanted to meet her. See her. Hold her. I needed the comfort she provided me so many nights, right now. In person.

I sent her an e-message. I invited her out to dinner. She responded. Quickly. I was glad. I didn't want to have to text her and I was too aggravated to call her. I read her reply. Maggiano's 8 p.m. sharp. I checked the time, 4:50 p.m. I sent a reply and set the date.

I logged off and lay down on my bed. On my back, one hand behind my head, another on my stomach, I watched the ceiling fan on low. Round and round. Each blade passing in rhythm. I closed my eyes.

I opened them what felt like minutes later. Glanced over at the clock. *No!! 6:50 p.m.* Damn it! I fell asleep. I hadn't even realized I was tired. I jumped up and ran into the bathroom. Started the shower, grabbed my toothbrush, spread some paste on, opened the door to my stand-alone shower and stepped in. I brushed my teeth and washed my balls at the same time. Spit, turned in circles to completely wet myself, lathered, rinsed and repeated. I quickly shut the water off, opened the door and jumped out to dry off. 7:15. *No! No! No!!*

I hated being late with a passion. I always considered it the most disrespectful thing you could do with someone's time. I was still wet when I put my pants on. No time for underwear. I slid one of my closet doors to the side and selected a black polo shirt. I didn't have time for buttons. *Sharlotte said 8 p.m. sharp! Tyson's Corner. That's at least 30 minutes away. Twenty if traffic is good.* I slid on some socks and loafers. I went into the bathroom for one last look over. Greased my head, sprayed some cologne in the air and walked through it. I left out of the bathroom, turning off lights on the way down to the garage. I grabbed my jacket, keys and checked the time on my cell phone. 7:24. I was moving.

I entered the garage, hitting the button on the wall to let the door up. I jumped in *Leslie*, put in John Legend..."*Want you to love me like you know the world's about to end, baby...quickly*"... I listened as he told me about the time I had left to love.

I zoomed down the beltway, weaving in and out of traffic, checking the time, doing my best to sing along with John and Andre as they gave me the *Green Light*. 7:40. I merged onto 495 and thought to myself that I should have been a NASCAR driver. 7:50.

I pulled into the parking lot of the Galleria. Zoomed up and down aisle's looking for a vacant spot. I saw a car pulling out just as I turned the corner to go down another isle. I zipped in. The car waiting to grab this spot will have to find another. Love waits for no one!

I jumped out, locked the doors with my keypad and jogged through the parking lot to the restaurant. There was a long ass line

95

coming through the double doors of the mall. Glad I called for reservations after logging of the computer. My jog slowed to a fast step once I hit the curb. I rang Sharlotte. She answered her phone elated.

"Hey! Where are you?" she asked.

"I'm here, about to get us a table. What's your preference, smoking or non?"

"Non, please."

I needed to know how much time I had to get seated so I asked, "Where are you?"

"I just parked. I'm on my way in now," she responded.

Sharlotte was a big flirt and an even bigger tease.

"What are you wearing?" she asked.

I laughed, remembering I'd neglected to put on underwear in my rush.

"Girl, get in here so I can show you! You'll know me when you see me. I'll be the one excited to see you and wearing a hard on!" I said.

She laughed and responded, "Ok, I'm coming. Bye!"

I loved the play on words and chuckled. She did too.

"Ok, bye and hurry!" I hung up.

I excused myself past a hoard of hungry people who cut their eyes at my arrogance and made my way to the hostess stand. I gave her my name and time, then slipped her a fifty. She nodded and said, "Right this way Mr. Richmond." She led me to a secluded booth in the right rear of the restaurant. Perfect. Not a lot of traffic and no noisy "gratuity included" parties near by.

As soon as the hostess moved from in front of the booth, I looked up and saw her. Sharlotte. Beauty. Love.

Janine Coaxum

She was tall, not too thin. Not too thick. Perfect. She had on this bad skirt that hugged her curves just right, all the way down to her ankles. Her top had a plunging neckline that had me curious. Our eyes met. I was entranced. Beautiful. *Manners, niggah. Manners. Get up, go meet her!* I slid out of the booth and walked towards her, meeting her halfway. I requested her hand. She obliged, placing hers in mine. It was soft, petite. Natural. No tips, no French manicure, no crusty cuticles. Her nail beds were soft pink and her nails were a good length and white as snow. I was impressed. She looked so familiar. I stared at her. As she passed in front of me to slide into the booth, those curves caressed me in all the right places.

My haste to get dressed left me without my armor. Sharlotte aroused me, turned me on. I leaned down as she made contact with the seat. I expected her to look in my direction, feeling my heat near her. She did. I kissed her. Soft and firm.

My mouth melted into hers. I breathed in her perfume. My kiss lingered longer than I had planned. What was supposed to be a peck, turned into passion. She tasted so good. Her lip-gloss was flavored. Peaches and cream maybe. I then realized that I had not been breathing and was quickly running out of oxygen. This woman had me holding my damn breath! MMMM!! I released her and stood erect.

I wanted her, bad. As she motioned for me to sit, I noticed that this had clearly been communicated to her. I wasn't embarrassed though. She needed to know. I smiled and slid into the booth across from her. We smiled at each other. I looked deep into her eyes and saw so much. I realized something. These were eyes that I had to spend a lifetime gazing into. There are some things in life that you just know. I knew from that night that I wanted Sharlotte to be my wife.

Chapter Thirteen
Sharlotte and JaRah

"Someone once told me, You never know who knows who"

Sharlotte

"It is so wonderful to finally meet you," JaRah said while examining me with approving eyes.

"Likewise! All I can do is smile. I'm glad you offered me dinner," I responded confidently.

"Later, I'll offer you dessert," JaRah said.

"You promise?" I asked.

I was flirting hard. I couldn't help myself. We went on like this for at least another 10, maybe 15 minutes. All the while sexual tension rising. Finally, the waiter interrupted our back-and-forth banter with the chef's recommendations for the evening. We ordered and went back to staring each other down.

JaRah broke the silence saying, "You look so familiar to me."

"I should! You've been staring at my pictures for weeks. Hopefully!" We laughed.

He continued, "So how long did it take you to get here?"

"About 25 five minutes. I was coming from Exit 3 off the beltway, in Maryland."

His face lit up. "Me too! Where do you stay?"

"Battle Creek? Next to the Metro station? You?"

I didn't think it was possible, but his face lit up even more.

"No way! I stay in Battle Creek too. I just bought a townhome over there about nine months ago! Small world!"

"Small world indeed," I chimed in.

We stared each other down even more intensely, wondering what else we had in common.

"So how was your day?" JaRah asked.

"Besides almost getting run over, it was great!"

"What? Please explain."

I went into the story of having a dog and how while taking her for a walk, a white Range Rover almost backed over me. All the while, JaRah's face was frozen. I was sure that the bread he was chewing was practically turning to mush in his mouth. His eyes were glossing over from not having blinked for the past two minutes. Finally I stopped telling my story and went straight into an interrogation session. Something was up. I hit JaRah with a slew of questions.

"Why do you look like that? Did I say something wrong? What are you thinking? Are you listening to me? Did you leave the stove on at home and just remembering or something? JaRah!"

He jumped in his seat. He took several gulps of water, wiped his mouth with his napkin, took a deep breath and began to speak. I leaned forward and listened.

Janine Coaxum

JaRah

It was so clear. I remembered where I had seen her...the BMW dealership walking her dog. I'd seen her a couple of times after that. Early in the mornings, walking her dog, all bundled up, guarded against the cold morning air. For a week or so, we'd timed our outings perfectly. She'd be out with her dog when I left for work. I recognized her by her dog, a black little thing with the fancy cut. Kaisheem had almost run her over this afternoon. I realized she was waiting for me to speak.

I swallowed my bread. It went down rough and dry. I gulped some water to assist, wiped my mouth and proceeded to tell her about the first time I saw her. I explained that I had just bought a new BMW at the dealership near our community. I told how I had seen her that day, walking her dog. She didn't believe me until I described the woman in the Italian leather and how I saw her trip when she noticed the woman. Sharlotte almost blushed with embarrassment. Her mouth fell open, "You were there, huh! Did you see her jungle breasts?" We laughed. I agreed with her on the "jungle breasts" and went on to tell her how I'd noticed her some mornings on my way to work. She smiled. I was ok.

Then I began to tell her about Kaisheem. I explained how we grew up and how I took care of him. She stopped me every so often to ask me a question or two. Where were we from, where did we go to school... I told her about Kaisheem's drug problem and his gold digger Olivia. Then I explained to her about the events this afternoon and apologized for Kaisheem's behavior. Her face lit up.

"No! That was your brother that almost ran me over! No way! Was he high?" she asked. That comment caught me off guard, which must have shown in my face. Sharlotte led in with apologies.

"I'm so sorry. That was rude and insensitive of me. I just cannot believe this."

"I know right!" I stated in agreement.

"Wait a minute. What model BMW did you buy?

"750. Why?"

"What color? she asked.

"Silver with wine leather interior."

"It was YOU! YOU took my parking space this evening!" she exclaimed.

Suddenly the guilt shifted and I felt bad for my behavior in the parking lot.

"My bad! I'm sorry about that. I fell asleep and woke up with only an hour to get dressed and get here. I was so excited about seeing you and I didn't want to be late. I hate being late with a passion," I said.

Sharlotte gave me a soft look that said *Mmmm hmmm. You're lucky I like you,* then she smiled letting me off the hook.

We ate and talked about so much over our dinner. We talked about her childhood, her career in the Army and her new job. Sharlotte was full of energy and passion as she spoke about her past times, her side jobs. She told me about her singing gigs in some of the local jazz clubs and her braiding clients.
Sharlotte even got into some of the horror stories from previous Internet dates. We laughed. We smiled. We enjoyed each other's company.

Sharlotte's phone chimed. Soft at first, then steadily getting louder. Her face changed.

"Don't get it," I suggested while she reached for her purse and pulled out her PDA.

"I just want to make sure it's not my best friend checking on me," she said.

She pressed a few buttons, silenced the equipment, placed it back in her purse and picked up her fork. She didn't eat, just played in her meal. She didn't look up. Something was wrong. The mood had changed just that quickly.

"Sharlotte, is anything wrong?" I asked softly. I didn't want to be intrusive. I thought about how I would react if my phone had gone off and it was a jump off or Kaisheem. Sharlotte looked up at me, her eyes glossy. She was on the verge of tears when she said, "I have a stalker."

Sharlotte

JaRah sat there staring at me, looking into my soul. I was breaking down. I felt as if my life was finally coming together, becoming complete and here was this nasty little reminder that I had problems. BIG problems. I had tried to ignore it, dismiss it, but I couldn't anymore. I felt myself beginning to cry. I tried to hold back, but no such luck. Tears came streaming down my face. JaRah had asked me was anything wrong. How could I tell him, nothing was wrong when everything was wrong? How could I tell him that I was finally happy and wanted him to be a part of my life, but oh by the way I have a stalker? *Just say it Sharlotte.*

103

So I did. I told JaRah I had a stalker. I cried. Not because I was scared of my stalker or afraid for my life. I cried because I didn't want this wonderful man to leave me alone. I had become exactly what I steered clear of. I had become DRAMA.

JaRah slid out of his side of the booth and slid in on my side. I was so embarrassed and said so out loud.

"What! No! Sharlotte, don't be. It's not your fault. Talk to me. Tell me what's going on."

I began, "It started when I moved up here for my new job in May. I never thought anything about it. It started with just somebody calling me, breathing in the phone, making off the wall comments and asking me questions. The calls always come from different numbers. Sometimes it says *Caller Unknown* and sometimes it says *Blocked call.* It's hard for me to conduct business because a lot of the calls I receive are from numbers not stored in my phone. I'm just tired. Please don't hold this against me."

"Hold it against you? Never!" JaRah put his arm around me and I fit perfectly under it. He held me close and stroked my temple.

"Why would I do that? Sharlotte, I consider us friends. I'm here for you. You need to know that."

I looked up at him and in that moment, I loved him.

Love is a very simple thing. The Bible tells us we should *Love thy neighbor* and says that *God is Love.* Going off of those two things, I had made up my mind that love was meant to make friends out of enemies and turn strangers into lifetime partners. Love was uncomplicated, until we complicated it. We tainted it with lies and deceit. I didn't want my love for JaRah to turn into that. So

I vowed to myself that I would tell him the truth. I would dish it, hoping he could take it.

JaRah

I sat there with Sharlotte. In Maggiano's Little Italy, while she poured her heart out, waiter's busted tables, people laughed and enjoyed good food and good company. I held her, caressed her temple and reassured her that I wasn't going to go running and screaming in the opposite direction. As she spoke to me, I cared for her more and more. I loved her more with every word. Sharlotte Swanson. She was strong, independent and savvy. Sharlotte Swanson. She was also weak and alone. She needed to be protected and I wanted to protect her.

My cell phone rang. Sharlotte got quiet. Wiped her face. She pulled away from me. I held her tighter. She relaxed in my embrace. My cell phone rang again. I reached across the table and grabbed my jacket. I felt my phone vibrating in one of the pockets. I held my cell, flipped the screen open and saw Kaisheem's name. I looked at Sharlotte. She gave me approval to answer my phone, as she saw Kaisheem's name as well.

I pressed the talk button and answered, "Kaisheem! Hey, man. What's up?" There was a lot of noise in the background, like he was driving with all the windows down.

"I'm on 95 South."

"What? 95 South! Where are you going?" Sharlotte pulled away to sit up as she reached for her water. I put my arm on the back of the booth as she did that. As she drank I watched her and listened to my brother.

"I'm losing it man. I can't do this anymore. I think I have a child out there somewhere and I have to find them. I have to find Tara... I need..."

"Kaisheem, man. Slow down. You're not making any sense! A child? By who? And who's Tara?"

Sharlotte stopped drinking her water and looked at me. She didn't speak. She just looked at me. She was waiting. She watched my lips as Kaisheem continued.

"I'm going to Georgia. I think she still lives in Georgia. Man, I'm so blown," Kaisheem laughed. "Me and Olivia hit the big dipper tonight! Whew boy!"

My mind raced as Kaisheem laughed and rambled about nothing. The big dipper. Where had I heard that? The big dipper. WAIT A MINUTE, the big dipper was a street name for weed laced with cocaine. I was really worried now. I spoke in a calm voice,

"Kaisheem, where exactly are you?" I asked.

"Man, I don't know. Virginia maybe. Yeah. Virginia. Past Richmond," he laughed.

Kaisheem was high. Sharlotte was still looking at me, eyes big as day. Kaisheem stopped laughing. It sounded like he was choking on something. I got nervous and yelled into the phone.

"Kaisheem! Kaisheem! Man, pull over! Stop driving and pull over right now. I'll come get you!"

He laughed and then said in a soft sullen voice, "Not savin' me this time. I gotta find Tara. Only she can save me. Tara. Tara...." His voice drifted out. I think he was hitting a dead spot, losing his signal.

I yelled, not caring about being in a restaurant, "Who is Tara! Kaisheem! Hello? Kaisheem!"

106

The phone call ended. I looked at Sharlotte and she saw the terror in my eyes. I was scared for my brother. She opened her mouth to speak but didn't say anything. This evening had turned out to be much more than either of us had bargained for. What was four hours had felt like four years. Sharlotte and I were more entangled in each other's lives than we realized.

SHARLOTTE

JaRah called Tara's name. He had called her name several times. My mind raced. I thought back to our conversation earlier. I remembered Tara's silence when I mentioned JaRah's last name. Did she know him? Did he know her? I had to know what was going on. Then I remembered her warning. *You never know who knows who.* Is this what she meant? Who did she know, JaRah or Kaisheem? I wanted to dial her up the moment JaRah said her name, but I needed more information.

JaRah closed his cell phone. He never took his eyes off of me the whole time he was on the phone. His eyes. They had so much fear in them. This was a delicate situation. Not at all the time for me to question him. I waited. I wanted him to speak first. Tell me what was going on so hopefully I could get the information I needed without having to ask him any questions. I was getting impatient; I opened my mouth, but couldn't bring myself to speak. Just then my cell phone rang. I broke our gaze and reached for my purse. I pulled out my PDA and held it in front of me, where JaRah could see. It was Tara.

Chapter Fourteen
JaRah Richmond, Sharlotte Swanson and Tara Steele

"I'm the new Mrs. Steele!"

Impeccable timing. Just when JaRah and I were about to burst at the seams from all the questions we had, the answer rang my phone. Tara's name popped up on the bright display. I looked at JaRah as he reached for his glass of water. He hadn't noticed the name.

I answered, trying to sound jolly, "Hey, girl! What's crackin'?" I did a piss poor job.

"What's crackin'? You ok?" Tara laughed, "Are you still out?"

"Why yes I am. I'm sitting here with Mr. Richmond right now." Silence.

I held the phone to my left ear, as JaRah was sitting on my left, and turned the volume up as loud as it would go. Tara spoke to me, "You must not be having that good a time if you answered your phone!" She laughed. I giggled a little and assured her this was not the case.

"We're taking a breather. I answered because I knew you were concerned earlier. I want you to know I'm ok." I said this with a hint of disdain in my voice.

Tara had a secret and I getting more and more pissed by the moment because I wasn't in on it.

"Sharlotte Nicole Swanson, may I trouble you for a moment of your time?"

My government name! Tara called me by my government name! This was serious. I looked over at JaRah. He was rubbing my back and content with his position. He grinned at me. I went back to my conversation.

"Sure, Tara. What's up?" It was on.

She had given me just what I needed to get things going. JaRah stopped rubbing my back and scooted in close to me. I looked at him and motioned for him to be quiet. He leaned in towards my ear and the phone and listened. Tara
had used my government name, which gave me a free pass to use hers in return.

Tara began, "I just got a call from John's new wife. She has my telephone number! *Sonofabitch!* You know I can't stand that bitch. Anyway, she called to tell me they moved to Washington, D.C. this summer and that he wasn't going to be able to drive all the way down here to Georgia to pick up the girls anymore. I said Bitch let him tell me that! Don't call my house with no ridiculousness! Oh, Sharlotte she pissed me off so bad! I'm sorry to call you with this, but I needed to talk to someone. I had to let it out."

"Girl, that's what I'm here for. It's all good! D.C. huh! Did you know they were moving?"

JaRah listened as Tara responded, "You know, John mentioned something around January, but he never confirmed anything. Sorry piece of crap. It's not like he sees the girls on a regular basis anyway. The visits are few and far between. All he did was collect a check from me. With the way our economy is, I don't know what the hell he did with that 'ole measly $300 dollars anyway. You can't even wipe your ass with that. He just want's to stay in my pocket."

I got bored with the conversation quickly and still had unanswered questions. I led in, "Hey girl! Let me ask you something and be honest."

"Uh, OK."

"Do you know JaRah from somewhere?"

"JaRah who? That guy you met up there? How would I know him?"

"I'm asking because when I told you his last name, you kind of acted funny."

"Acted funny? I didn't act funny. I told you I'm concerned for your safety."

"Bitch, don't play me. You know something and you're not telling it." Silence. JaRah leaned forward to look me in the face. He mouthed *Who is this?*

The waiter walked over and left the check on the opposite side of the booth, smiled and walked away. JaRah and I looked up at him, only for a second, smiled and then dismissed him from our world. I quickly took the pen from the leather jacket that held the check, snatched a napkin from near the salt and pepper shakers and scribbled *best friend Tara Steele.* I slid JaRah the napkin as I listen to Tara confess it all.

Tara

I told myself *the charade is over: I'm tired. Kayla is 10 now and that is 10 years too long to be holding on to secrets and lies. Besides, I didn't have to ever see Kaisheem again if I didn't want to...even though I did.* I told Sharlotte everything. I started with how the last name Richmond rung a bell with me. I remembered Kaisheem first, JaRah later. I hadn't ever met JaRah, so his name didn't stand out in my mind. I told her how we met in college and how I got pregnant before graduation and married John so that Kayla would have a responsible father. I told my best friend she was sitting next to my one true love's brother.

I heard her sigh and swallow. "Girl!" she said. That was all she had to say. Sharlotte the queen of come backs was speechless. I sat in my upstairs bedroom, curled up in my bed with a thousand pillows on it. Jay Leno was on the boob tube and Sharlotte was speechless on my phone.

"So, John is not Kayla's father!"

"Girl no! She don't even look like him."

"Does John know that Kayla's not his daughter?"

"You know sometimes I think he does, but then other times I think he hasn't got a clue. He doesn't care much about either, so if he did know, he has a funny way of showing it. I mean you'd think he would favor Shauna over Kayla, but he doesn't. He doesn't favor either one of them."

"Girl!"

"Will you stop saying that! You're way more articulate than that, Ms. Master's Degree!"

My joke helped to lighten the mood, but there was nothing funny about the way my life was falling apart. I was tired. Tired of doing the single parent thing. Tired of being alone and tired of not having love. I spoke to Sharlotte, "I'm getting off the phone now. I'm tired." I heard a commotion. It was hushed and shushed. "Sharlotte, you hear me? I said I'm getting off the phone now."

"Wait! Wait, Tara, I gotta tell you..." More hushed commotion.

"Tell me what, Sharlotte? I said I'm tired now!" I was getting annoyed with whatever was going on over there on her end of the telephone. Then it hit me. She was still at dinner with him! Had she put me on speaker phone? Did she tell him who she was on the phone with? Damn it Sharlotte!

I knew Sharlotte well. She wasn't slick at all. She probably had the volume turned up on the phone, so JaRah could listen from the other side.

"Sharlotte!" I yelled.

"What? Wait a minute don't go; just hold on a second," I said.

"I'm hanging up!"

Just then I heard a male's voice. "Hello, Tara? My name is JaRah. Kaisheem is my brother." Silence.

I sat in my bed silent. I didn't know what to say. I didn't want to talk to him, and Sharlotte gave him the phone? What did he want? I didn't say a word. I just listened.

"Hello? Tara? You there?"

"I'm here."

"Listen, I know this is awkward seeing as I don't know you, but my brother does. He's on his way down to see you."

"WHAT?" I jumped up in my bed, pillows hitting the floor on all sides. My heart raced. Had I heard him right?

"How is Kaisheem coming to see me? He doesn't even know where I live," I said.

"That's the problem. That's why I begged Sharlotte to put me on the phone. My brother...Kaisheem is well...he's..."

I helped JaRah out, "He's high as a kite. Ain't he?" Silence.

JaRah's response, or lack there of, to my question confirmed one of my worst fears. Kaisheem hadn't changed. The man on Sharlotte's phone let out a sigh. Then he spoke,

"Yes. He's high. He called me about 30 minutes ago and was rambling on and on about needing to find you and having a child out there somewhere.....I need to know can...."

I tuned him out. His voice trailed off and I think I dropped the phone. How did Kaisheem know? I guess I wasn't as smart as I thought I was all these years. I wondered if he had known all these years. I got out of my bed and went into the bathroom leaving the phone on the bed. I felt nauseous. Sick to my stomach. I looked at myself in the mirror. *See what lies and deceit will do to you.* Kaisheem was coming to find me. Coming to find us! I wasn't ready to have that talk with Kayla. I couldn't upset her whole world like this. Not to mention trying to explain to Shauna the concept of half siblings. She's only five!

Wait a minute! What have I done! No! No! No! I washed my face and went back into my bedroom. I opened my door and looked down the hall towards the girl's rooms. They were sleeping quietly. Thank God for small miracles like the telephone. I forgot I was still on the phone.

I sifted through the covers and found it, but the call had ended. The only thing on the screen was a picture of my girls. The date and time displayed across Shauna's smile. *Mommy, can't you move it?* I recalled her asking me. I smiled and put the phone on my nightstand. 11:30 p.m. I was tired, but I knew I wouldn't be able to sleep. Kaisheem was on his way to find me. Richmond. High as a kite.

My cell phone rang. I picked it up. *John Steele.* Was he calling to apologize for his bitch wife calling me and stepping out of place? I'd hoped so. I answered, "What?"

"Don't what me!"
It was her. Stephanie, that bitch.

"You've got some nerve calling me at this time of night. Have you lost you're mind? There is nothing you and I need to talk about at..."

"Shut up! I'm looking at your best friend's CLS 500 and it's sittin' on four flats!" Stephanie exclaimed.

"What?"

"Trick, that's right. I got your attention now. Don't I?"

"I don't believe you. You're crazy!"

"No, I'm the new Mrs. Steele Bitch! You better get that through your skull. Mess with his money and you mess with me! Don't ask us for anything ever again or everyone you know will pay!" She hung up.

That crazy bitch hung up on me! What the hell was she talking about? This was just way too much drama for one evening.

Knocking pillows out of the way, I found my house shoes. One foot at a time, I stepped into my memory foams and shuffled past toys and shoes downstairs to the kitchen. Nothing in the refrigerator held my interest. I opened the cabinet, pulled down a bottle of Johnny Walker. I poured a glass, took a swig, and it burn slow as it went down, then I went to the fridge for a chaser. I wouldn't be able to stomach Johnny straight tonight. I grabbed a small bottle of Merlot, poured a little more Johnny to fill my glass. I left everything out on the counter and headed back upstairs.

I set my drinks down on my nightstand and noticed I'd had a missed call. I pressed buttons and pulled up the missed call list. Sharlotte had called. Why was John's wife calling me so late? She had lost her mind. I knew I'd have to cuss that bitch out and I was feeling right for the job. First, I called Sharlotte back. I dialed her number. The phone rang once and then gave me a fast busy signal. I pressed the END button.

I took a swig of Johnny and a swig from my small bottle of Merlot. Took a swig of that to cool the burn. Dialed Shar again. It rang. She answered.

"T! What happened to you? JaRah said he was talking to you and you just put the phone down!"

"My bad, I had a moment." Truth be told, I was having a moment right now. I was feeling good. Guzzling alcohol and preparing to cuss that bitch, the NEW Mrs. Steele, slam out.

"Are you ok?"

"Oh, girl, I'm good."

"Yeah 'cause you done fixed you a drink!"

We laughed. She was so right. I continued to laugh while Sharlotte spoke.

"JaRah is worried about Kaisheem. Kaisheem doesn't know where he's going. JaRah just got off the phone with him. Kaisheem's on 85 south now, nearing Charlotte, North Carolina.

JaRah wants to know can he give you Kaisheem's number, so you can call him. Maybe talk him off the road. He's really flying. Doin' like 100. He's in no shape to continue on like this. He'll wrap himself around a tree or worse kill someone else. Tara. You hear me?"

I sat sipping and listening. Then I realized, I'd have to face the music. I remembered what John had said that day at the courthouse. *What's done in the dark ALWAYS comes to light.*

"Sure. Give me his number."

"You're gonna call him, right? Please Tara. JaRah is really worried."

"Yes. Yes. I will call him. Just as soon as I call this bitch back and cuss her out. I giggled at the thought. Pleasure before business. "Do you know she threatened me! She was talkin mad junk on my phone just a couple of minutes ago."

"Come on T. This is serious!"

"Oh I know! You don't have to convince me! I'll call him. Then I'll call you back. Oh and Sharlotte, check your ride. That bitch said it was sitting on four flats."

"What! That bitch is crazy! How would she even know where I am? Does John know I live up here now?"

"I may have mentioned it to him a month or so back. That bitch is bluffin. There's probably not a damn thing wrong with that house payment you drivin. Just text me Kaisheem's number. I'll call."

"Alright. I'm sending it right now. I love you, Tara. Don't forget to call me back. Everything is gonna be alright." With that, Sharlotte hung up.

I thought about calling that bitch back, but decided against it. I'd save that for when I had a clearer head. Besides, I needed to talk to John and figure out what Stephanie was referring to when she said, "Mess with his money and you mess with me."

I know that little $300 I was paying him hadn't affected them. I received the text with Kaisheem's number and stared at it. I thought about what I would say. I looked at the pictures of Kayla and Shauna across my dresser. Kayla looked so much like Kaisheem, more so now that she was getting older. There was no denying it. She was his child.

I selected the number in the text and confirmed that I wanted to dial it. It rang. It rang again. I was going to hang up on the fourth ring. I had already made my mind up that I wasn't leaving a voicemail. Third ring.

"Hello?"

"Richmond?"

"Tara?"

I heard him sniffle. "Richmond, are you crying?" I asked.

"Yes! My life has been so awful without you.

"Richmond, please, stop at a hotel. Get some rest. We'll talk in the morning."

"How did you get my number? How did you find me? I've been looking for you, but I could never find you!"

"Richmond, I was never far away. Please, just stop at a hotel. Will you do that please?"

"For you Tara, anything. Just answer me this. Do we have a child?"

"Her name is Kayla."

Kaisheem broke down. He sobbed and let out a moan. This was the second time I'd known of him crying. I heard a car lay on the horn in the background.

"Richmond! Richmond!"

"I'm ok, it's cool. I'm getting off in Rock Hill. I'll call this number back in the morning."

"OK," I said.

"Tara..."

"Yes, Kaisheem"

"I love you."

"I love you too, Kaisheem."

We hung up. I took a deep breath. It was hard enough to love someone when they were perfect, let alone through all their imperfections. Kaisheem was a druggy, a smart one at that. I loved him just the same. Now my love was coming home. I dialed Sharlotte to let her and JaRah know Kaisheem would be alright. No answer. Not even voicemail, which was odd. I hung up, waited a few seconds. The Johnny Walker and Merlot were kicking in and I was getting sleepy. I pressed the button to redial her number. It went straight to voicemail. I left her a message and figured she had a bad signal. I put my cell phone on vibrate, placed it on the nightstand and turned off the television. As my cheek hit the cool pillow, Johnny Walker and the Merlot sweethearts sang me a lullaby goodnight.

Chapter Fifteen
Sharlotte Swanson on Stephanie Steele

"It's that good 'ole Shit Happens Theory"

Maggiano's was closing down. People were collecting their "to go" boxes and giving hugs and kisses while they put on their jackets. Waiters were bussing tables and straightening linen napkins. JaRah's cell phone rang. He flipped it open. We both looked at the screen. Kaisheem. He answered and spoke to his brother in a soft low voice. I reached for my purse to check my cell phone. My battery was dead. I looked back over at JaRah. He was deep in conversation with his brother. I waited patiently for the news.

JaRah ended his conversation and closed his phone. He shifted in the booth, leaned in towards me and caressed my face.

"She called him. He's at a hotel in Rock Hill, South Carolina for the night. He said that Tara promised she'd talk to him tomorrow."

I closed my eyes and breathed in JaRah's scent. Then I felt his lips. His kiss consumed me. My mind wandered. I knew Tara's number by heart and could have very well called her from JaRah's phone, but I didn't want to move. I wanted to stay in this moment. I thought of Love. I loved Tara. She loved me. We weren't honest with each other. I loved my parents, but never told them the whole truth about everything in my life. I'd loved other people in the past and had deceived them somehow. I wanted so badly NOT to have that with JaRah. I didn't want love's deceit to creep in, settle and get cozy between our hearts. I knew this was going to be work, but I was so willing to put in the effort. JaRah was ready to match me.

We pulled away from each other slowly. I opened my eyes. His were still closed. I smiled. *How cute. He kisses like we're in junior high.* He slid out of the booth and grabbed his jacket. I grabbed my purse and did the same. He extended his hand to help me up. Such a gentleman. We collected our boxes and preceded to the exit, arm in arm. Step for step. Then I remembered what Tara had told me.

"Damn! I gotta check my car!"

"What! What's wrong with your car?" JaRah was annoyed, as if he couldn't take anymore drama this evening.

"Stephanie! Tara told me her ex-husband's new wife threatened to have flattened my tires. I don't think it's true, but still. I'm not putting anything past her. From what Tara has told me about her, she's trifling and vindictive."

"Where did you park?" JaRah asked scanning the parking lot.

"I'm down on the end." I motioned for him to follow me. He suggested that we get in his car and drive over to mine since he was parked closer. I agreed. We left the sidewalk and walked straight down the aisle to his 750.

Mmmmmm, it was nice! He pressed the remote to unlock the doors then opened the passenger side door for me. I turned to him and said, "Why thank you Mr. Richmond." I slid into his plush paradise. As he motioned to close my door, he gave a response that left me speechless.

"My pleasure, Mrs. Richmond."

Mrs. Richmond? Me. Sharlotte Swanson, Mrs. Richmond. Mrs. Sharlotte Richmond. My heart pounded with excitement at the thought of it! I leaned over and opened his door for him, being careful not to hit the car parked beside him. He thanked me and got in, shifting and adjusting himself like he was missing some part of his ensemble. He backed out and I directed him to where my CLS 500 was parked. All four tires were still inflated. False alarm from a crazy bitch. I sighed a sigh of relief and relaxed in the seat.

JaRah let out a giggle. "You really thought something might be wrong. Didn't you?"

"Hell yeah! Stephanie Steele is crazy. I met her twice at Tara's place. Her ex-husband had the nerve to bring that crazy bitch with him to pick up the girls one weekend."

I told JaRah to park in the space one over from my car and cut the engine because this was going to be a long story. JaRah did as I asked; seemingly interested in the tale I was about to tell, so I began.

"Tara's ex-husband's name is John, John Steele. He and Tara were married for just about seven years. They had not long ago divorced when Tara and I started working together, which is how Tara and I met. The divorce was fresh because they were still going to court over custody and visitation issues while we went through orientation at our job. Well, John was seeing this woman, Stephanie, long before the divorce was final. Tara thought he'd been seeing her for some years, but said she didn't really care, as long as John continued to handle his financial responsibilities."

JaRah interrupted, "Woman, are you gonna get to the good stuff anytime soon?"

"Give me a minute; I'm long winded!"

"I see." He let me continue.

"So, anyhow, John married Stephanie before the ink could dry on the divorce decree. This particular weekend I was chilling at Tara's crib like I did on so many occasions and John pulls into the driveway with this bitch profiling on the passenger side. Her hand dangled out the window with a big 'ole diamond catching every sunray available. She wore shades like she was too cool or common folks. Tara and I were sitting on the front porch doing what nosey black women do in a ghetto bourgie neighborhood. When this bitch has the nerve to get out of the car, walk up to the porch and park herself at the bottom of the steps. Then Stephanie takes off her shades and asks us 'Where dem kids?' We thought it was funny because first off, the girls are far from being 'DEM KIDS' and secondly Stephanie was an idiot if she thought Tara was actually going to let her girls go with her and John after having made her request like that."

I chuckled as I continued to tell the story. "We laughed. Oh! We laughed so hard at that ignorant sounding bitch. We must have laughed for a good three to five minutes. Stephanie just kept repeating over and over, 'Well, where are they?' And we just kept laughing. After we regained our composure, Tara got up from her chair on the porch, walked to the top of the steps and stopped. I wasn't sure what she was going to do, which made me a little nervous. I've got her back no matter what, but we're too damn old for cat fights. Tara walked down the steps, past Stephanie over to the driver's side and leaned in to talk with John. Meanwhile, I'm left on the porch with his bitch starring me down...like I'm the one that used to screw her husband. I got tired of the starring match and just asked the bitch if she had an eye problem. She tried to get loud with me and started talking all kinds of noise. I quickly shut that down. I stood up and walked over to the steps. She dared me to come down them. I did. Then this bitch swung at me!"

"What!" JaRah was into the story, his face in awe.

"Yes! The bitch swung on me."

"What did you do to her? You must have said something that hit a nerve?"

"All I did was ask her if she had an eye problem. The bitch is crazy, certifiable. Anyhow, she swung on me. I leaned back and almost lost my balance since I was coming down steps. I wasn't trying to catch a charge for assault or attempted murder so I taunted her. I told her to try again and she did. She started in with the windmill, classic!. I ducked and dodged and laughed at her. She really looked ridiculous."

"You were playing with her! That's just wrong Sharlotte." JaRah and I laughed hard because it was wrong.

"I couldn't help myself. The crazy bitch went off on ME 'cause she couldn't get at Sharlotte. By now, John had jumped out of the car to come and restrain Stephanie. The girls were on the front porch laughing, and Tara was doubled over in the front yard with tears in her eyes.

Neighbors were beginning to gather in clusters and it was generally becoming a field episode of that Springer show. John got Stephanie in the car and strapped her in with her seatbelt. Oh! Stephanie was HOT! Everybody was laughing at her. Somebody even caught it on tape and put it on YouTube.com. I'll have to show you. *Huh-larry-us.* Since that day, Stephanie has had it out for me. Oh she can't stand my black ass." I leaned back in my seat and took a breather from laughing, JaRah did the same.

I reminisced and continued on, "One year, Tara and I ended up at a workshop where Stephanie was a presenter. Disaster. Stephanie damn near lost her job trying to have Tara and I arrested for stalking her."

"What? Naw!"

"Yeah! She was convincing! Almost had Tara and I believing we really were stalking her. She called the police at the convention center and had us "detained" for questioning. The only thing that saved us was our registration, which was done by our supervisor months before Stephanie had been asked to be a presenter for the workshop. Crazy bitch."

JaRah sat back in his seat again. He had been leaning towards the steering wheel, listening intently to me the whole while. I reached for the door handle, while he spoke.

"Damn! She IS crazy."

I stepped out of JaRah's paradise, *Leslie.*

"Yeah, lucky me. Huh?"

"And you never did ANYTHING to her? Why does she hate YOU?"

"Sometimes there is no why. You know JaRah, I believe in this theory. I call it the 'Shit Happens Theory'. It's a theory that speaks to occurrences or events that cannot be explained."

I closed his door and got in my car. JaRah followed me closely as we headed back to our community. I plugged my phone up to the car charger and sent JaRah a text...*YOUR PLACE OR MINE?*

Chapter Sixteen
The Invisible

"It doesn't even matter who I am. Just call me the background."

I'm nobody. I'm that kid in elementary school that you never noticed in the class pictures. The kid in junior high who never got picked for kickball. I'm that plain teenager in high school that had no signatures in my yearbook. I'm nobody. I'm a filler, a void between one point and another. I don't have any friends and I don't have any family except an older brother. He takes care to remember me, calls me from time to time and makes sure I'm still living.

Our parents died when my brother, 15, and I, 4, were sent into the system. Foster home after foster home proved to be our only means of socialization. I learned the world through suitcases and blank walls. I never had a real home, always one change of clothes away from being packed, ready to go on to another home.

Every set of foster parents I had encouraged me to talk more, interact with the other kids in the home. I never had much to say. I didn't trust them, didn't trust anyone. I didn't like to play games or draw. In fact, I didn't take pleasure in many of the activities children are forced into. I never played outside or even inside for that matter. I just sat and watched. That's what I was good at. That's what I took pleasure in. I watched people, watched the things they would do. I'd often stare at people and never speak. It would make people feel uncomfortable, so I learned to be coy about it.

When I graduated from high school, my foster parents at the time asked me what I wanted to be. I told them I didn't know and had never thought about it. They asked me who I saw myself as. I told them I saw myself as a nobody. They talked to me for hours on end about self esteem and tried their best to explain to me that everyone is somebody and that I too have some purpose. I told them it didn't even matter who I was.

"Just call me *the background*," I said.

When I woke up the next morning, they had packed my bags and bought me a plane ticket to go live with my brother in Maryland.

My brother is only my brother biologically. Being 12 years apart made it almost impossible for the foster system to keep us together, so we never lived in the same homes. We kept in touch through letters. Some of the foster parents I had actually drove me to see him once or twice, on a birthday or holiday. My brother and I didn't speak. We had nothing to talk about. On those trips to see him, I would just sit and watch every one. I'd watch how they all hugged one another and gave each other praises. It all seemed phony to me. I watched my brother guard himself and make fake happy faces. He wasn't happy. He didn't believe these people were happy either.

When I arrived in Maryland, he had a room prepared for me in the attic of a co-op building he rented. I took it gratefully. We still didn't speak. Nothing had changed. He took me the following week to tour the area, showed me where the local markets were and made sure I had all the important telephone numbers and then he left me to be on my own. I had done well in high school and made good grades. I wasn't dumb, far from it. I took an interest in school. That's where the people were. School was the only familiar constant in my life, so I went back.

I enrolled at the University of Maryland College Park and took a few courses. I wasn't interested in any particular major and there weren't any counselors willing to work past my social awkwardness to find a major that best suited my abilities. So, I majored in Human Resources. Ironic, I know, but it was an easy course load and I learned to fake my way through all the classes that required me to interact with the living. One thing I wasn't expecting was the world it introduced me to: mass amounts of people.

I had people to look at and visually dissect. People and their information. Where they come from, what they weigh, eye color, hair color, height, address, telephone number...the possibilities for dissection go on and on. Finally, I had found a place to be invisible amongst people.

I fought my way through a couple of interviews with some government agencies and secured a position as a Human Resource Assistant before graduation. I left school still unnoticed, still a nobody, but with a renewed spirit in the world. I had a goal, a purpose. I would find the perfect person to spend the rest of my life watching, looking at, dissecting. I would find someone who would intrigue me and keep my attention until I had taken apart every inch of his or her being, examined it and looked it over twice. That's all I wanted. Just one person.

What I've learned from watching people, is that they hide the truth, but if you look close enough, watch long enough, you can always see through the lies. Then and only then can you love them for who they are. That's what I'm looking for, watching for, waiting on. One person to love. Love. That's a funny thing. Before I decided to find my one person, I had never considered love. Love was always an emotion that disappointed me, let me down over and over again.

What is love anyway? Really. Most everyone says I love you, but what they're really saying is, I love you as long as...I love you as long as you don't change. I love you as long as you don't ask me any questions that require me to be honest. As long as you continue to lie to me, deceive me and never tell me the truth. I love you as long as you love me in return. I love you as long as you stay attractive. I love you as long as you don't hurt me. I love you as long as...as long as you stay sane, make sense.

I never believed anyone who said they loved me. It was mostly because they didn't know me. That was fine because I never knew them either. I never said I loved them back. I never tried to deceive anyone with love. I never will. When I find the one, that's when I will finally say it. I'll say it and I'll mean it. Then, I will die for it. Die for it. Dying reminds me of a conversation I had with a psychiatrist down in Georgia once. Dr. Steele, how can I forget Dr. Steele. She was interesting to watch. She had a lot to hide. So many stories, so many lies. I could tell by the way she made eye contact with me, always trying to out stare me. Always tapping her pen and swiveling in her chair.

I had a session with the good doctor before I left the foster home, my guess is to make sure I didn't have any adjustment issues with the transition. Dr. Steele asked me if I'd ever thought about hurting myself or others. I was silent, as usual. I pondered the question, thought about my answer and told her yes. I explained to her that I thought of hurting myself and others all the time. Isn't that what we do when we love? Seemed like the right answer to me. Dr. Steele thought otherwise.

She made it clear to me that she was referring to bodily harm that would 'cause injury or death. I looked at her, looked at the lines on her face and saw the pain and unhappiness in her life. How could she ask me about bodily harm or death when she was clearly hurt from love and dying slowly inside?

Dr. Steele didn't get it, she didn't understand. With all her degrees and training, she was clueless. I watched her as she wrote on her notepad, not realizing she had asked me a series of questions I didn't answer. Finally she asked me if I often thought about death. Death? Death.

I watched Dr. Steele as she glanced at the clock on the wall behind me, then down at her notepad. I told her death was a mirror and that it's reflection is what we see in each other everyday. That one put her over. She pulled out a small pad, scribbled something, tore off the top piece of paper and handed it to me. It was a prescription for an antidepressant. Here I was, being completely honest with the good doctor, trying to enlighten her even and she writes me a prescription for an antidepressant.

I stood to leave. Dr. Steele looked through me and wished me luck in the future. I never filled that prescription. She had stirred thoughts in me, thoughts about love and death. There was absolute truth in both. You realize both in the end. That was then and this is now. I have found love, discovered the truth. All I have to do is plan it just right. Timing is everything in situations like this. My love will realize soon enough, that my love will not deceive.

Chapter Seventeen
Everyone

"Goodnight, Mr. Richmond. Goodnight, Mrs. Richmond."

JaRah

I sped up. I was speeding at 85 miles per hour just to keep up with Sharlotte. One thing I love more than fast cars is a woman driving one. Sharlotte had quickly become the object of my affection and I was chasing her. I pulled up beside her and taunted her. She let down her window just a bit, the night air whipping loose strands of her hair around. She smiled and stepped on the gas. I grinned as she took off. We neared our exit off the beltway and slowed to a modest 55 miles an hour. She took the exit first; I followed like a lost puppy. Her Mercedes CLS 500 looked as good from behind as Sharlotte did. They were a perfect match.

We pulled in to the complex and headed toward my townhome. Sharlotte let down her window to wave me around. I pressed the button on my garage door opener and slide past her into my garage. Leslie was a tight fit. That got me thinking about tonight and what I was hoping to get into. Then I messed myself up. I started thinking about our future and what I wanted for the both of us. I loved Sharlotte and our relationship thus far had been untainted by the confusion of flesh. I decided then that we would go inside, relax and talk some more. I needed to know that Sharlotte and I really were on the same page.

Sharlotte

I slowed and let my window down to wave JaRah around so that I wouldn't block him from his garage. He drove past and as his garage door went up he slid in slowly, that big body Beamer barely fitting inside. I was falling in love, deeper and deeper with his every action, his every word. I pulled up in his driveway and cut of the engine. JaRah was at my car door before I could step out, extending his hand. Such a gentleman, finally I had hit the chivalrous jackpot. He helped me out of my car and held my hand, leading me into his garage and through the door into his house.

His soft hands led me up the stairs into his living room. Suddenly, I was nervous all over again. I was curious, but more than that I was thinking too much. I was thinking about having a relationship with this man...one that would last the rest of our lives. I was thinking about marriage and children and finances and consolidating household dishes, furniture, friends, closet space, color schemes and bedroom sets. I sat down on the love seat and looked up at him. We looked at each other.

"I don't wanna have sex yet," I blurted out.

"Good! Me neither! What we have is different, special. I'd hate for us to ruin it by moving too fast," JaRah responded.

I let out a sigh of relief. Thank you sweet Baby Jesus for putting us on the same page. JaRah kept talking and I tried my best to focus on what he was saying, but my mind was once again racing. I looked around his living room while he rambled on about lust and the flesh and confusion. He had great taste. His living room set was a burgundy suede, which was complimented by deep cherry wood feet. His coffee table was round and had a map of the world on it. His lamps were antique and also of cherry wood. He had gidgets and gadgets of all sorts in various places.

I liked his style. His things would compliment mine very well.

"Sharlotte! Well, what do you think?"

Uh oh, I hadn't been listening. I did that from time to time with people.

"I'm sorry JaRah. I was in another world. You know, soaking in the whole evening. I wasn't listening. I apologize. What were you saying?" I asked.

JaRah giggled. Thank goodness he found the humor in the situation. I was relieved.

"Never mind, baby. It's not important. What it is, though, is late. You are more than welcome to stay the night with me. Actually, I insist." JaRah's words were like warm chocolate on my tongue, sweet. His gaze swallowed my soul. How could I resist.

"Take me to the bedroom," I said.

He placed my hand in his. I stood, and he took me into his arms. We held each other for what seemed to be hours. Squeezing and rocking from side to side, our hearts beat in sync.

He led me up the third flight of stairs to a massive bedroom filled with decorative Asian art, Japanese swords, and sculptures of black bodies. I was impressed by his style. He had two large ceiling-to-floor window treatments that must have cost hundreds. Each wrapped in silk colors matching his bedding.

He didn't have much furniture, just a California king size bed, a nightstand and an armoire. JaRah picked me up like he was carrying me across the matrimonial thresh hold and gently placed me on his bed. The only light in the room came from a small lamp on his night stand. His eyes sparkled in that light.

He removed my left Jimmy Choo black patent leather pumps and placed it on the floor. Then he took my toes between his fingers and squeezed them. I closed my eyes and relaxed with pleasure. This man was rubbing my feet! He was definitely a keeper. He stroked the bottom of my foot with a smooth slow rhythm, being careful not to tickle me. The he followed suit with my right foot. I was in Heaven. He undid the clasp on the side of my skirt. I lifted my bottom up off the bed and assisted him in easing it off. I could tell by the change in his breathing that he was pleased with what he saw. I sat up and pulled his shirt over his head. His chest was amazing. I began to undo the button on his pants when he stopped me.

"Wait. I'll have to handle this one," he said.
My facial expression must have told him that I was both confused and intrigued.

"I was in such a hurry to see you tonight that I went commando."

We giggled as he excused himself to his master bathroom. I took off my top, pulled back the covers and slid into his bed. The sheets were crisp and smelled new, just bought from the store no doubt. JaRah emerged from the bathroom looking like a king. He posted up in the doorway, his arms holding the top of the door frame. His muscles tensed. I could see that his body had plans for me opposite of what we had discussed. I smiled and motioned to the excitement below. I know, right! We just had a talk about that, but he wasn't tryin' to hear what I was sayin'. I smiled as he walked over and climbed in the bed. I was exposed. He was looking at me. All of me. His lips parted and he let out a sigh.

"I can't do this, Sharlotte. I don't trust myself. I'll go downstairs and sleep on the couch. You stay here in my bed," he said.

"Are you serious? No way! I didn't agree to stay over here and sleep by myself! JaRah, look. I'll help you. We can do this together. Give me a T-shirt or something" I pleaded with him.

"Ok, a T-shirt. I think maybe I can do a T-shirt and a pillow between us and some socks on your feet...maybe a doo rag on your head. Don't you sleep with a doo rag on your head?" he asked.

I laughed hard and said, "Yes, JaRah. I normally sleep with a doo rag on my head, but I'm still sexy!"

He opened up his walk-in closet, which contained the bulk of his dresser's, opened a top drawer and pulled out a white oversized T-shirt, closed the drawer and closet door then walked back over to the bed.

"JaRah, what is this?" I laughed.

"It's a T-shirt! Girl quit trippin'. You thought I was playin'?"

JaRah handed me the t-shirt, and I slid out of bed to put it on. Over my head the sheet of a shirt went and once I finally adjusted the massive piece of cloth over my body. I slid back into bed. JaRah had already gotten cozy and tucked his pillows down along his side.

"JaRah! Come on now. The pillows really are a bit much."

"Girl, I'm as serious as a heart attack. I need some fantastic intervention or I'll be all over you, all...night...long," he said.

Mmmmmmm! This man was serious. I settled in next to the pillows between us, leaned over the "fort" to kiss him goodnight and rested my head on the one pillow he left untouched.

He said good night to me as if we were already husband and wife. "Goodnight, Mrs. Richmond," he said.

"Goodnight, Mr. Richmond."

What seemed like an hour later proved to be 10 hours later. We had slept well into the afternoon. I opened my eyes and stretched, not realizing where I was. I looked over to my left and there he lay, sleeping like a baby, JaRah Richmond. It felt good to wake up and see him lying there, peaceful and drooling. I looked out the window at the view of the wooded field behind his townhome. Peace.

Everything seemed at peace. Then I remembered Cocoa. I had to get home and let her out! My poor baby! I had totally forgotten. Time had gotten away from me. I jumped up and scrambled for my clothes. JaRah lazily sat up in bed.

"What are you doing? What time is it?"

"Cocoa, I completely lost track of time. I gotta go let her out and feed her. I know she's just about through with me," I said.

"Oh, that's right. The little black fancy thing. Call me in a couple of hours. OK?" JaRah laid back down.

"OK, baby, I will."

I walked around to his side of the bed and gave him a kiss on his forehead. He looked so adorable, all curled up in the fetal position. All that was left to complete the pose was for him to suck his thumb. You'd have thought I had put him to bed last night. I hurried down the first flight of stairs to the second level and almost bust my tail once my feet hit the wood floor panels. I hadn't noticed them last night. Nice, but dangerous. I looked back as I scurried towards the third flight to see if I had left any scuff marks with my Jimmy Choos. No marks. I was good.

As I made my way over to my apartment building, I thought some more about JaRah and Kaisheem and my best friend Tara. Funny how we were all connected. As I thought about it all, I could see the features in Kayla's face, features that were definitely from the Richmond's side. Kayla and Tara. I needed to call my best friend and find out if she had met up with Kaisheem yet. I'd do that just as soon as I got myself together.

No sooner than I thought that, Tara was ringing my cell phone. To answer my phone, I had to juggle my purse, my clothes and my keys as I entered my apartment.

"Hey, T! What's up? My battery went dead last night. Everything go OK?" I dropped everything in my hands and let Cocoa out of her kennel. She nuzzled my legs and forgave me. I hooked her up to her leash, went back out of the apartment for a brief walk and listened to Tara let out a sigh.

"Girl, where do I begin? Kaisheem called me early this morning, like around 6 a.m. He and I talked on the phone more than two hours. The whole time we were on the phone, either John or Stephanie or both of them bitches were calling me on my other line, not wanting anything in particular except to work my nerves. Apparently John has been doing some 'other' things with their money and lying to Stephanie about it. Get this, instead of him telling her what has really been happening to the money, John tells Stephanie that I cut back on the alimony payments. Stephanie is such an idiot that she doesn't even know I don't have to pay John alimony anymore."

"Dang, girl! So the court documents went through and he doesn't get that money from you anymore. What in the world?"

"I don't know and I don't care. I told them both to leave me out of whatever financial woes they're going through."

I headed back into my apartment just in time for my phone to start beeping.

"So what about Kaisheem, T? Hold on I need to plug up my phone (insert elevator music) Ok, now what about Kaisheem? Where is he?"

"He's right here, sitting in front of me and watching me talk to you."

"Wow! Is he all up in your grill?" I laughed.

"I heard that!" Kaisheem said.

"You got me on speaker phone!"

"No girl, you're just that loud!"

We all laughed and everything seemed to be coming together. Tara told me Kaisheem wanted a blood test to be sure Kayla was indeed his daughter and Tara had no problem with that. Tara said that Kayla saw Kaisheem pull into the drive way and had announced his arrival as, "Mama, some man who looks like he's kin is here." Children have a way of just coming right out and saying it. Kayla took the news pretty well, referring to other kids in her school who had similar situations with both step and biological parents. Tara sniffled and told me she hadn't realized how fast the girls were growing up.

"What about Shauna? How did she take the news?" I asked.

"Shauna? What news? Shauna said she always knew something was wrong with her sister." We laughed.

Shauna was a comedian, always the first one to the punch line, no matter the situation. In the midst of all this was Kaisheem.

"Since he can hear me, what about Kaisheem? How is he doing in all of this?" I asked.

Kaisheem answered, "I'm great! So much better now. Tara is more beautiful than ever and the girls, Oh! The girls are wonderful. It just feels really good to finally know. You know?"

"I know," I said.

"OK, girl, I'm going to get off this phone and feed my children and long lost lover, if you don't mind."

"Not at all, T. I'll catch you later on. I love you!"

"I love you too, Sharlotte. Bye!"

"Bye!" We hung up.

It was Saturday and everything seemed as if it were happening so fast. Just last week, JaRah and I were sending e-messages across the Internet, flirting with the idea of one day meeting. Last night I slept in his bed and listened to him breathe, then kissed his forehead this morning.

My world was spinning in a good way. I looked at the clock. It was almost three o'clock. I figured I would go for a walk and take Cocoa along with me, then come back to shower and call JaRah. That was the plan, until my cell chimed. I checked the screen on my PDA. It was a text message from an unknown number. I could see the beginning of the text, which read *come outside and...*I selected the option to view the entire message, which continued...*walk with me to Heaven.*" I deleted the text and got nervous. The phone calls were one thing, but a text message was something new.

I decided against going for a walk and called JaRah. He answered his phone on the third ring, sounding half sleep.

"Hey, baby. You at home?" he asked.

"Yes and I need to come back over. Do you mind?"

"Naw, no way! Come on. I need to get up anyway. Have you heard from your best friend?"

"Yeah, I just talked with her not too long ago. She had Kaisheem there with her. He met Shauna and Kayla and they're all having a *Come to Jesus* moment. Kaisheem is going to have a blood test done, just to be sure. They're one big happy family...sort of."

"Wow. I still can't believe I have a niece and by your best friend!"

"I know. It's a lot to take in."

"Have you eaten? Maybe we can grab something in a little while?"

"That sounds good. Can I bring Cocoa?"

"Sure! Bring her; she's house broken, right?"

"Yeah, she's good. Thanks JaRah, I'll be over in a few minutes. I'm just gonna grab some things."

"Ok, baby, I'm here." We hung up.

This feeling of fear was strange and new to me, but it felt warranted. Something suddenly didn't feel right. I packed an over night bag and some things for Cocoa, loaded up my car and drove back over to JaRah's. On my way out of the parking lot, I noticed that same old beat up Oldsmobile was still sitting at the far end of the parking lot, but it had been moved. It's new position being more within the guidelines for parking in the complex. It was backed in and between the lines. There was something freaky about that Oldsmobile, the way it stood out from all the other cars in the parking lot. I couldn't put my finger on it, but it just didn't sit well with me.

I turned my attention back to JaRah and headed toward his place. As I pulled into his driveway, I thought to myself that we should pray as soon as I got inside and thank God for each other. That's just what we did. JaRah and I sat down in the living room, held hands and prayed. I never believed old folks when they said you could sense that something was coming, until that very moment. As JaRah and I held hands, with our heads bowed, eyes closed and hearts open, I knew my life was going to change.

Chapter Eighteen
The Background

"...see the color of the name tag?"

Human Resources is an interesting term for the work that I do. Instead of managing resources for humans, my job sings more to the tune of the exploitation of human beings for capital. I like my job, so I don't speak up or rock the boat while the people I work with are robbing the government blind. They come to work late, use company resources for their own benefit and even take home things like paper clips and staplers.

I know of a few real estate agents who have taken three hour lunch breaks to show clients properties. Bit by bit, they're causing our department budget to expand. It doesn't bother me not one bit. I just stand off to the side and watch. I don't say anything at the coffee machine or offer up any gossip at the copier about who's sleeping with whom. Oh no! I just stand to the side and watch.

Watching is what I do, and because I do it so well, no one ever notices me. I have successfully become the background. I'm a filler, and extra in the movie of my life. I don't have stylish hair or clothes, so there's nothing to compliment me on. I don't have a funny walk or a particular smell, so you'd never notice me in passing. My name is as plain as the come, so not even that would make me interesting on a sheet of paper.

Two years, two long years of being the background suddenly came to an end when she spoke to me. She noticed me and spoke to me. Not just a whisper in passing. Not an "excuse me" just to get by me in a crowd. She spoke to me, looked me in the eye and said, "Hello, my name is Sharlotte Swanson, and you are?" Sharlotte Swanson. A beautiful name for a beautiful woman. She was tall, had pecan tan skin, almond eyes and pearly white teeth. Her hair was pulled back into a ponytail and she wore pearl earrings complimented by a single strand of pearls around her neck. She had on a grey suit with a blue pinstriped collared shirt and black heels.

Sharlotte Swanson had noticed me, come across the room to speak to me, looked me in the eyes and saw deep into my soul. She had exposed me and made me vulnerable. I became visible when she did that. Others in the room could see me, could see that I had been watching them.

One person said to Sharlotte, "Oh no! That's the person from HR, not a new employee."

Another person chimed in, "Yeah, see the color of the name tag."

Sharlotte smiled at me and said, "Oh! I'm sorry. This activity is confusing. I saw you looking at me and thought you were a new employee too."

I was exposed, naked in a room of humans who had signed up to be exploited. She waited. She stood in front of me and waited. Even after others had explained to her that I was no one, the WRONG one, she still waited for me to speak back. I was frozen. I don't even think I blinked. Then she said, "I must have caught you off guard, huh! It's cool. You're not even supposed to be playing this game anyway. I'll talk to you later!"

Later, later, later, later. Sharlotte said she would talk to me later. Suddenly the room was full of haters, full of folks who would love to date her.

I rambled this tune in my head for hours on end after that June morning orientation. Sharlotte Swanson had come all the way across the room to speak to me. ME! She had seen me, noticed me. I excused myself from the meeting room, ran down the hall to the elevators, took one floor up and headed down the hall to my cubicle. I scurried past the buffalo at the watering hole and zipped by the pigeons squawking in the copier room. I logged on to my computer and opened the employee database.

Sharlotte Swanson. Sharlotte Swanson. Got it! I pulled up her information, scanned through to her address and telephone number. I then Googled her address to see where she lived. I scribbled down her number and directions to her address on a notepad and then quickly logged out.

I had found my one person to love. Now I had to figure out how I was going to get her. My extension rang and startled me. No one ever called me. I looked at the display to see *Union City Hospital*. It was my brother. I answered, "Yes Bradston."

"Hey. I need for you to come and pick me up from work tonight. Ok?"

"Fine, Bradston."

"What's up with you? You sound like you're in a good mood?"

"Oh, just another day at work."

145

"Ok. If you say so. Listen, since you refuse to join civilization and get a cell phone, you'll have to park and come up to the fourth floor. That's Behavioral Health, ok. Just ask for me at the Nurse's Station"

"Yes, Bradston."

"Ok. So I'll see you around eight."

"Eight o'clock it is."

"Thanks. Bye."

"Goodbye."

My brother was an orderly on the crazy unit at Union Hospital in downtown D.C. He loved his job and loved his crazy people even more. I loved to watch them. Some of them had rituals, moving in the same patterns and making the same gestures over and over. Others couldn't hear you over the voices in their heads. When they did hear you, they freaked out, thinking they were hearing voices.

Later, later, later, later. Sharlotte said she would talk to me later. Suddenly the room was full of haters, full of folks who would love to date her.

A tap on my cubicle wall brought me back to my present situation. I looked up to see a huddle forming at the cube across from mine. I stood at my desk, watching them all gathered around, bent over, whispering awes and ohs. Then I walked away. No one invited me over to look and that was fine with me, but something felt different. I almost felt curious about everyone's amazement.

Sharlotte had awakened something in me. As I walked down the hall to the elevator, I noticed that more people noticed me. People looked back at me when I looked at them. People smiled in the middle of their sentences and others threw up their hands to wave at me.

What is this? What has she done? Suddenly I felt angry and betrayed. The elevator doors opened and I got on. I scooted past several people to stand in the back corner of the elevator.

A man in the middle turned around and spoke to me, "Hey! How's it goin?"

I blew up. "How's it going? Do I have a sign on me somewhere that says *PLEASE SPEAK TO ME?* Don't talk to me., none of you, ALL of you! DON"T TALK TO ME!"

DING! The elevator doors opened on the third floor and everyone got off. I heard one woman headed toward the stairs saying that she hadn't signed up to work with crazy people. The folks who were waiting to get on decided to wait on another car. The elevator doors closed. *What has she done? What has Sharlotte done?* I felt like Sharlotte Swanson had removed an invisible cloak that I had worn all my life. I felt heat in my chest and my palms began to sweat. I had to find her. I had to find her and make her undo what she had done.

As I made my way back around to the June orientation session, I noticed a small group of people sipping soda's across from the door. I paused before going back into the meeting room and watched. They sipped and chatted about being new to the area and how difficult it was to find their way around. One person suggested taking the Metro before driving. Another person suggested getting a navigation system for their car.

A coworker came out of the meeting room and ushered the small group back in. No one noticed me. It must have been a fluke, a freak occurrence. I took in a deep breath and followed the group into the meeting room. Once inside, I stood next to a counter that ran along the entire side of the room. Still close to the door, I scanned the crowd for Sharlotte and found her, sitting with her legs and arms crossed, listening intently to the presentations we bore every group with.

I watched her. She didn't notice me. She shifted in her seat. I shifted in my stance. She never turned her head to look my way. The presentation finished and a new presenter came through the doors as the previous went out. Everyone turned their attention to the entrance and exits, but no one, including Sharlotte, looked at me. I was back. My cloak was back. I was relieved.

The June orientation session ended and new employees scattered to the wind. Some went home, while others went to their sections to meet their new coworkers. I watched Sharlotte. I followed her. She went to the cafeteria and got a cup of hot tea (two Bigalow apple cider teas, eight sugar packets and about an ounce of cream). Then she stopped by the Credit Union ATM and withdrew four $20 bills. I followed her to the elevators and lost her as she got on. Several people laughing and talking covered Sharlotte's floor request. No worries. I knew I could look up her cubicle number in the employee database.

I took another elevator up to my floor, went unnoticed to my cubicle. I logged on to my computer, opened up the database and did a simple search. There it was, right in front of me on my screen. I had everything I needed. I had Sharlotte Swanson's telephone number, social security number, birthday, bank account information, address, cubicle number, her in case of an emergency contact and work schedule. I had it all.

I logged off the computer and shut everything down. It was five o'clock, time to go home. I joined the hustle and bustle in the hall to the elevators, down to the parking garage, broke out of the pack and headed towards my brother's Oldsmobile. It had seen better days, but it still ran. I knew it was good for cutting off in traffic so I decided to leave straight from work and head over to the hospital.

As I started out of the garage, I noticed all the faces in their cars passing me by. Foggy windows and loud music made for an exciting scene. I turned out of the garage onto New York Avenue and the Oldsmobile cut off. Expletives and middle fingers were all the help I got. I sat and tried the engine several times. Then I just waited. I let everything settle down and tried the ignition again. Ten minutes later the Oldsmobile cranked up. I gave it some gas, put it in drive and merged angrily with the rest of the traffic.

The Oldsmobile cut off on me three more times before I made it to Union Hospital. It was 7:47 p.m. when I pulled into an employee parking space. I decided to leave the car running. I got out and slammed the door. Anyone who thought they wanted this piece of junk could have it. I walked into the hospital and went up to the fourth floor. I went to the nurse's station and asked a male nurse, who was smacking on a piece of gum, to call Bradston Jones.

The nurse, not even looking up, replied, "Who's paging?"

"Pat Jones."

"And you are?" he asked.

"His relative."

Finally, the nurse looked up at me and gave me a nasty look for being smart. He picked up the telephone receiver, dialed three numbers and said, "Orderly Jones to the nurse's station, Orderly Jones to the Nurse's Station" then let the receiver fall back down into place. I walked over to the dayroom. There were people watching infomercials, people visiting patients, people staring off into space, out windows and people starring at other people. I noticed a phone in a cubby on the wall next to the television. I walked over and sat down in the chair. I wanted to call Sharlotte.

I pulled out the paper I had written her number on and noticed scribbles on the desk and on the wall around the phone. Scribbles of various things like words, letters of the alphabet in both Greek and English, telephone numbers and doodle faces.

I pulled a pen out of my coat pocket and moved the telephone to the side. I wrote Sharlotte's telephone number on the desk with instructions: *Call this number for a good time.*

"What are you doing?" someone asked.

I jumped, grabbed the phone, put it over Sharlotte's number and turned around in the chair. It was Bradston.

He asked once again, "What are you doing? Did you write something?"

"What?" I asked trying to sound as if I didn't hear him.

"I said...never mind. Are you ready?"

"Yes, Bradston," I said.

"Let's go."

I followed my brother out of the dayroom and past the Nurse's Station, all the while keeping my head low for fear that what I had done would show on my invisible face that was visible today for just a while. We got out into the parking lot, and I led my brother to the car.

"You drive," I suggested.

"Cut off on you, huh?" he asked then laughed. I didn't think it was funny.

We got into the Oldsmobile and left the hospital. Bradston rambled on and on about work and new people to the unit, both patients and employee's. I halfway listened as I thought about Sharlotte.

Later, later, later, later. Sharlotte said she would talk to me later. Suddenly the room was full of haters, full of folks who would love to date her.

Chapter Nineteen
The Oldsmobile

"Just then...everything went black."

I woke up Monday morning at 6:50 a.m. I was late. Late for work and late for my period. I dragged myself out of the bed, sliding JaRah's arm from around my waist and replaced my spot with bed sheets and pillows. It had been three months since our first date and we were still going strong. I shuffled to the bathroom, turned on the light, and thought back over the last couple of months while I washed my face and brushed my teeth as I thought:

Tara and Kaisheem are working things out. DNA test came back 99.99%, Kaisheem is Kayla's father. John and Stephanie are doing what they do best, which is to annoy folks with their drama and I'm pregnant. The whole celibacy thing went out the window after the second month.

Too much fun in the leaves one Sunday afternoon proved to be the catalyst for a tumultuous night of passion. Running through the house, upstairs, downstairs, locking bathroom doors and eventually taking the screws off of door handles, we tried our best, but were no match for the love we felt growing between us. JaRah and I had passionate, tearful sex and now, as I wiped my face, I had to decide what course of action to take.

I left the bathroom and opened up JaRah's closet. I flipped the switch on the wall and walked to my spot in the middle. I had gradually brought over a few things. A few pair of shoes, some suits for work and some junk clothes to relax in. My mind raced.

I wonder if JaRah knows. He knows we didn't use protection. He knows he climaxed and didn't pull out, and he knows I'm not on the pill.

One leg at a time, that's how pants go on. I looked out of the closet at the clock. It was 7:10. My eyes went to JaRah, who was slowly rolling over, grabbing pillows and covers. He let out a huff and let a leg dangle off the side of the bed. I giggled at him because he was going to be late too.

"Baby, get up," I said.

"No," JaRah mumbled, his faced mushed in a pillow. I laughed and walked over to the bed. While buttoning my shirt, I leaned over JaRah and kissed an exposed area of his lips.

He brought his face from under the pillow to give me a kiss from the corner of his mouth.

"Alright now, don't start none, won't be none," he said.

We smiled at each other. JaRah rolled onto his back and off the covers, sat up, and planted both feet on the floor. He turned and watched me as I put on my earrings and watch.

"You're pregnant."

I froze, staring at JaRah. Speechless, my arms dropped down by my side. JaRah stood up from the bed and walked around toward me. Tears formed in my eyes as JaRah took my hand. He caressed my cheek and held my face.

"I know you're pregnant." He kissed my lips as a tear fell from my eyes. JaRah kissed the tear in midstream.

"How do you know?" I asked.

"I saw the box in the trash, dug a little deeper and found the test, all three of them. It's gonna be OK. We'll just have to get married sooner." I cried harder.

"Get married? Sooner?" I asked.

JaRah got down on one knee, still holding my hand in his.

"Yes, Sharlotte. We've got to get married sooner. So will you marry me? Tomorrow?" he asked.

I giggled, "Tomorrow? Hmmm, let me check my schedule and see what I'm doing tomorrow. Tomorrow! YES! I'LL MARRY YOU TOMORROW!"

JaRah stood up and held me. He held me tightly and didn't want to let go. He held me as if he would never hold me again.

"JaRah. Please, baby, not so tight. I can't breathe!" I pleaded and chuckled in the same strained breath.

JaRah loosened his grip but still didn't let me go. He leaned back to look at my face.

"You are so beautiful, Mrs. Richmond," he said.

"Why thank you, Mr. Richmond. You're not so bad yourself!"

JaRah released me, but only for a moment. In his mind, he was going to have the rest of his life to hold me tight. I kissed JaRah on his forehead as he turned to go into the bathroom and wished him a good day at work.

We promised each other telephone calls and yelled our *I love yous* throughout the house as I went out the door and JaRah started the shower.

I got in my car and turned the ignition. My Mercedes CLS500 had an aluminum cased engine that ran off synthetic oil, so I didn't have to sit and let it warm up. I turned on the seat warmer, front and rear defrost and windshield wipers to break up the frost so I could see. As I let all instruments work their magic, I glanced in the rearview mirror and saw a plume of smoke coming from a dingy white car.

Squinting, and adjusting my rearview mirror to assure I was seeing this clearly, I peered between the white lines of frost on my rear windshield and saw that same old beat up Oldsmobile parked at the end of the street. My cell phone chimed. I jumped and dug through my purse. It was JaRah.

"Is everything OK? I see you just sitting there."

"I'm OK but do you see that dingy white Oldsmobile down the street? That's the car I was..."

"What Oldsmobile? I don't see any dingy white car."

I checked my rearview mirror. Sure enough, the car was gone.

"You missed it. It was just there. It's the car I was telling you about."

"Well, it's gone now. Did you see who was inside?"

"No. It was too far away."

"Let me jump in the shower and get back to you. OK?"

JaRah called me back a minute later, and we talked for the remainder of my way to work. Once I arrived at New York Avenue, I announced my arrival to JaRah. We said one more set of *I love yous* and got off the phone.

I drove into the parking garage and looked for a convenient parking spot. I parked my car and got out. Just then everything went black.

Chapter Twenty
The Plan

The garage has cameras...but not all over."

I got her. I got her early Monday morning. Much earlier than I had planned, but still, I got her. I waited outside her boyfriend's house and left just before she did. Bradston's Oldsmobile almost didn't make it. I slept in the car so that I would be on time to beat Sharlotte to work. When I woke up it was 6:50. I was almost late. The car wouldn't start. I tried the ignition at least 10 times.

Finally, around 7:30 a.m., it started. I had to sit and let it warm up, which wasn't a problem, but I was already 30 minutes behind schedule. Sharlotte's morning routine put her at work by 7:45 a.m. I had to hurry. I saw her come out of the townhome as I was just about to pull off. The gear shift was stuck. I couldn't get it to shift into drive. *No, no, no! Not today. Today is a special day. Not today! She's in her car about to pull off and I'm not there yet!*

I tried it one more time and it shifted into drive. *That was too close!* I drove out of the complex and raced towards Pennsylvania Avenue. I had to hurry. No doubt, Sharlotte would get to the office right after I would. I knew where she liked to park in the garage, so I had to get there before her in order to put myself in position.

I had already taken the week off, so no one was expecting me in to work. It was going to be just me and Sharlotte, forever. I sped through traffic, in and out of lanes, as fast as the Oldsmobile would go. I turned down Florida Avenue and made a right onto New York Avenue. *Just a couple of blocks and I'll be in position.*

Later, later, later, later. Sharlotte said she would talk to me later. Suddenly the room was full of haters, full of folks who would love to date her.

I was through waiting for later. I turned into the parking garage and drove to the basement. I parked in a far corner and got out of the Oldsmobile. My plan was to wait until I saw Sharlotte pull into a parking space, run up behind her once she got out and hit her over the head with a lead pipe fitting I got from my brother's basement. I decided against that, as I didn't want to do too much damage. I needed her intact and I didn't want any blood in the garage. No finger prints. No blood. No evidence at all.

Instead I decided to use ammonia. I went into the backseat and pulled a bottle of ammonia from a shopping bag. I poured some onto a dish towel, being careful not to inhale the strong smell. Then I saw her car. She had driven down further than I had expected. Not part of the plan. Why had she done that? There were plenty of good spots near the elevator! Now I had to run and get close to her car before she got out. I ran down the garage after her car and hid myself between two parked cars three spaces from her Mercedes. I peeked from around the parked cars and walked in a crouched position to her passenger side bumper. The ammonia had me a little dizzy and light headed.

I went around the front of her car to the driver's side. Just as she closed her driver's side door, I stood and covered her mouth and nose with the dish towel. She inhaled a good bit of it and struggled a little before she passed out. She fell at an awkward angle and her head hit the side view mirror of a van parked next to her Mercedes. She went down hard. I felt kind of bad because I didn't want her to be damaged in any way. I knew when she came to, that injury was going to hurt.

I looked around to see if there were any spectators. I peered into every vehicle parked in the vicinity. There wasn't a soul around. I saw two cars headed in our direction and got nervous. I had no idea how long she would be out, so I grabbed her leg and drug her in front of her car.

The two cars passed. I pretended to be searching my pockets for something. I had my black toboggan on with my scarf wrapped around my neck several times. I wore my black Isotoner gloves and my big oversized Outfitters camping jacket. The cars passed and I grabbed her leg once again. I positioned her between her front bumper and the wall she had parked in front of. I had to hurry. I ran back to the Oldsmobile and got in, hoping the whole jog that it would start. I turned the ignition. Nothing. *Please,please!*

Later, later, later, later. Sharlotte said she would talk to me later. Suddenly the room was full of haters, full of folks who would love to date her.

I tried the ignition once more and the engine turned over. I backed out and drove in reverse to the space where Sharlotte had parked.

I got out and went to the front of the Mercedes where I had left Sharlotte. She wasn't there. She wasn't there! I looked down the garage to my left and saw break lights of cars pulling in and searching for parking spaces. No Sharlotte. I looked to my right and saw someone stumble into a car and almost fall over. I jumped in the Oldsmobile and put it in reverse. I mashed on the gas and sped towards her. She turned and looked back at me just as I hit her.

I slammed on the breaks as soon as I felt contact with my bumper. I put the car in park and got out, hoping I could just pop the trunk and lift her in, but she was half way under the car. I got back in and pulled forward a little, got back out and grabbed Sharlotte by her jacket collar. She moaned a little. The trunk was locked. I needed the keys. *No, no, no!* I had to turn the car off to open the trunk! This hadn't been part of the plan. I had forgotten that the Oldsmobile didn't have a latch to pop the trunk, only the hood.

Sharlotte moaned and was beginning to fight me. I reached in my pocket for the dish towel, but it wasn't there. I had dropped it. *No, no, no!* Just then a car came around the corner and stopped behind me. The headlights were so bright. I couldn't see the driver. Sharlotte leaned against the Oldsmobile and I threw my arm up to shield my eyes from the headlights. The driver honked the car horn, and I motioned for the driver to go around. The car sped off through the garage and down to the opposite end.

One thing in my plan I knew I could count on was for folks to mind their own business. These days, people are nosey, but no one wants to get involved in someone else's mess.

Sharlotte let out a scream that shocked me and caused me to lose a little bit of my bladder. In one motion I turned toward her and slapped her. I slapped her so hard, I heard her neck snap. Her body went limp as she fell back toward the trunk and slid down the back of the car. Down by the tail pipe she lay. My pants were slightly wet. I shook my head and got myself together.

I went around to the driver's side, turned the ignition off and walked back to the trunk. I had to hurry. This was taking a lot more time than I had planned. I put the key in the trunk and opened it. I grabbed Sharlotte's jacket
collar once again and shoved her in the trunk. Then I grabbed her arms and legs and tucked them all in. I closed the trunk, but it popped back open. *What now!* Her jacket was hanging over the latch. I tucked her jacket inside the trunk and slammed it just as I noticed the reflection of the siren light on the security patrol vehicle as it came around the corner.

"Hey, buddy! Keep it moving. Find a space to park or leave the garage."

"Yes, officer." I walked around to the driver's side and got in. I went to put the keys in the ignition and realized I had left them in the trunk. I got back out the car and the Security Officer was standing at the trunk, watching me.

"You okay there?"

"Yes Officer." He held up the car keys and said "You left these back here." I walked over to him and took them from his hand. "Thank you Officer." I turned and got back in the Oldsmobile, put the key in the ignition and hoped the engine would turn over. It did.

The car started right up. I looked in my side view mirror and watched as the Officer wrote on a clipboard. I put the car in drive and made my way out of the garage. I checked my rearview mirror several times to be sure no one was coming after me. The garage has cameras, but not all over. I had planned on Sharlotte parking in one of the spots she usually parked in, which didn't have cameras. I had NOT planned on Sharlotte making her way down to the end of the garage we were. I hadn't checked that end and I wasn't sure if the cameras covered it.

I turned out onto New York Avenue and made my way over to North Capitol, got on 395 and headed towards the beltway. I had found the perfect little shack off of Route 1 for us and that is where we were going. We fought morning traffic the whole way and ended up sitting on the beltway for about 40 minutes before we hit Route 1.

I turned off of the main road onto a dirt road and followed it for about a mile. As I drove along, I realized that I had not tied her up. I pulled over into some high grass, turned the car off, and removed the key from the ignition. I got out of the car and made my way to the trunk.

When I opened the trunk, Sharlotte was covered with all sorts of miscellaneous items Bradston kept in there. She was among his jumper cables, old gym clothes, tools, a tennis racquet. I grabbed a sock and stuffed it in her mouth and covered it with duct tape.

I pulled her upper body out of the trunk and leaned her against me while I wrapped her arms and waist with more tape. While she was still unconscious, I pushed her back in the trunk and then closed it.

I got back in the car, put the key into the ignition, and hoped, with each breath, that it would start up. The engine hesitated a little, but it turned over. I took a deep breath and smiled to myself and drove off. *Later, later, later, later...*I sang.

I finally reached my destination. It was far off a path in the field, our little shack. I chose this place for us to spend our days and nights together, forever. I turned off the dirt road and drove down the gravel path that led through the field to the shack. The Oldsmobile had bad shocks and this wasn't improving matters. Everything in the car bounced and rocked. Things slid off the seats and onto the floor and the radio even went out. No matter, I had my Love in the trunk.

It was early Monday morning and the sun was just beginning to come up. I pulled up to the shack and drove around to the side not exposed to the road. It was much colder in the shadows. I stopped and put the Oldsmobile in park, turned off the engine and sat for a moment.

I wondered if I had been inconspicuous enough. *Had I looked like I was up to something when that security officer approached? No worry, I had my Love in the trunk...in the trunk...Later, later, later, later. Sharlotte said she would talk to me later.*

I grabbed a flashlight from the floor of the passenger side and got out of the car, excitement growing inside of me. This was my purpose in life, to be with Sharlotte. This is what I had been waiting for, watching for. All those years in foster homes, all those years in school, all those years surrounded by people, invisible and alone. All those years had come to an end.

I took a deep breath and walked around to the trunk. I put the key in the lock, turned it and the latch let loose. The heavy metal trunk popped open. I clicked on the flashlight and accidently shone it directly into Sharlotte's eyes, which opened wide and then shut out the beam from the flashlight.

She turned her head from me like I disgusted her, like she didn't want to look at me, like I wasn't someone who was attractive and interesting. No matter, I had my Love in the trunk. I tucked the flashlight under my left arm and grabbed a hold to her feet. It was awkward trying to pull her out of the trunk and not drop the flashlight, so I didn't tug hard.

Later, later, later, later. Sharlotte said she would talk to me later. Suddenly the room was full of haters, full of folks who would love to date her, I hummed aloud as I tried to get Sharlotte out the trunk without dropping the flashlight. Tug, tug, tug. Out she tumbled, onto the ground. She hit the ground hard, her eyes closed.

Chapter Twenty- One
Missing

"They do weird things when they get like that."

8 a.m. "Monday morning rush," I said aloud as I hit the gas pedal and then the break pedal. I picked up my cell phone and began to unlock it. A car horn blew and as I looked up, I slammed on the brake and to avoided hitting the car in front of me by a few feet. "Damn it!" I shouted. Then I laid on my horn out of frustration and put down the phone, thinking *Sharlotte is pregnant. I wonder how long she's known. I should have been more careful. I'm not ready for kids....neither is she. I need to call her.*

More horn blowing and cursing interrupted my thoughts. I adjusted my rearview mirror, let my seat back a bit and relaxed. This was going to be the longest drive to work ever. My cell phone rang, and the display read Kaisheem.

"Hey, man. What's up?"

Kaisheem spoke loudly as he rode in a car with the windows down.

"Not much, man. I'm going to be heading back up to D.C. in a few days. Things didn't really work out down here with Tara, but it's all good. We both agreed that it was a good try. We've just grown apart. She did get me to talk with an addiction specialist. I found out a lot about myself. I got a long road ahead of me. How are you and Sharlotte?"

"What? Man, I can barely hear you. Say that again." I said.

"I asked, HOW ARE YOU AND SHARLOTTE?"

"Oh! We're good. Both of us got up late, so this morning was kind of hectic. She's pregnant."

"What! I didn't hear you. Say that again."

"You heard me. I said she's pregnant."

"What are you going to do?"

"Marry her," I said with confidence.

"Marry her?" Kasheim asked with bewilderment.

"Marry her. I was going to propose anyhow. Now we'll just have to move everything up and go to the courthouse sooner."

Kaisheem listened to me curse in traffic. He laughed and said, "Marry her, huh? Daddy, huh? Wow! I leave you alone for a couple of months and look what you get yourself into. You done went off and got yourself a family!"

I laughed and replied, "No different from you! How's my niece doing anyhow?"

"Kayla is great! She is really a character. She's smooth with her game like Pops, but patient and caring like Tara. She's smart like me. I hope that's all she inherited from me."

We talked on the phone about this and that until I arrived to work. As I pulled into the parking lot of the firm and pacified *Leslie*, I ended my conversation with Kaisheem. While getting out, I noticed a cell phone car charger on the floor of the passenger's side. I leaned over and picked it up.

Sharlotte's car charger. Let me call her. I know she'll need it, I said to himself.

I dialed Sharlotte's phone and waited. Silence. No ring, no message. I ended the call and pressed the redial button to try calling her again. The call went straight to voicemail. *Her phone must be dead,* I thought. I threw the car charger back on the floor, closed the door and headed inside.

"Good morning, Mr. Richmond," my receptionist sang.

"Good morning, Ms. Baker."

"Do want your messages from the weekend now or should I give them to you in a few minutes?"

"I'll take them now. Thank you, Ms. Baker."

As I reached to retrieve my messages, my phone rang. I drew back my hand and searched my satchel for my cell. Clumsily I withdrew it from my bag and fumbled with it. It was Kaisheem again. I exhaled a deep breath.

"Is everything alright, Mr. Richmond?"

"Yes. I'm just...if Sharlotte Swanson calls, please just put it directly through to me. OK?"

"Yes, Mr. Richmond."

"Thank you, Ms. Baker."

I extended my hand again and shakily took my messages from the receptionist. *Whats wrong with me? Something is not right, but what?* Suddenly a wave of panic came over me. I unlocked my office door, dropped my bags at the door, and rushed to my desk.

My stomach was in knots as I picked up the phone and dialed Sharlotte's work number. As it rang, I glanced at the clock on his desk. It was 8:47 a.m.

Her voicemail began: *You have reached the desk of Sharlotte Swanson. Please leave a brief message including your contact information and I will return your call at my earliest convience. If you require immediate assistance please press zero at the tone.* At the tone I pressed zero and the phone rang.

"Procurement Branch, Ms. Talbot speaking. How may I direct your call?"

"Yes, this is JaRah Richmond. I'm trying to reach Ms. Sharlotte Swanson."

"Ms. Swanson is not in just yet. May I take a message?"

"Actually I spoke with her this morning and she didn't mention to me that she would be in late. Does she have a meeting scheduled? If so I can check back with her afterwards."

"No. She has an open schedule this morning and should have been here by now. Is there a message I can deliver upon her arrival?"

My heart shifted in my chest.

"Yes, please let her know that Mr. Richmond will be expecting a call from her this morning." I gave the receptionist my contact information and hung up.

With everything that Sharlotte had going on, I was lost in a sea of possibilities. The harassing phone calls she was receiving had gotten worse over the last month. Random calls at all hours of the night. Bizarre comments and requests had Sharlotte on edge. The Oldsmobile she kept seeing parked in her complex caused her concerned, and she had spent most of her nights at my house. Now, I was worried that things may have escalated.

I reached for my cell phone once again and dialed Kaisheem's number. Rubbing my eyes and squeezing my forehead, I waited for my brother to answer.

"Hey, man. What's..."

"Kaisheem, listen. I think something is wrong. Have you spoken to Tara this morning? Do you know if she's talked to Sharlotte?"

"Whoa, slow down. I just left Tara before I talked to you. I don't think she has talked with your girl, but I'll ask. What's going on?" Kaisheem asked.

"Man, I'm worried. Sharlotte is not at work yet and you know she's had somebody playing on her phone since she moved. I don't know what to think," I said.

"You don't think she just went off somewhere to get her head together? I mean she is pregnant. They do weird things when they get like that."

I was silent. Slightly angered by Kaisheem's comment, yet somehow amused.

"There's something not right about this. She was freaked about seeing this car this morning before she left. Her car charger is in my car, so if her phone is dead...awe man. Something is just not right," I said.

"Ok. Ok. Just stay calm. You're at work right?

"Yeah, man," I said.

"Ok. I'll call Tara and see what's up. Then I'll call you back. Just stay calm."

"Alright. I'll try. Just hurry up, man. I'm really worried."

"I got you. Sit tight."

We hung up and I opened up a file on my desk. I scanned the papers, but saw no words on them. My mind wandered. My thoughts were scattered to the wind. *What if she did just leave? I don't think she would just leave. She seemed fine this morning, a little nervous about telling me, but she was happy when she left. That car...that Oldsmobile. What did she say about that car? A white car...dirty...damn! I can't remember.*

A knock at my office door brought me back to the here and now, back to my worries and fears.

"Come in," I said to the visitor.

The door opened slowly and a freshly manicured hand gripped the back panel. A woman of about 40 and in great shape took a few steps into my office. I looked at her and thought of Sharlotte. This woman's curves were well pronounced in her business suit, much like those of Sharlotte's.

"Mr. Richmond, good morning. My name is Shayla Denise Simmons. We have an appointment to discuss account contracts."

"We do. Ms. Simmons, would you mind having a seat in the waiting area, and I will be right with you," I said.

"Of course. Take your time," she said.

Following, Ms. Simmons's exit, I got a return call from Kaisheem.

"Hey, man. Has Tara heard anything?" I asked.

"I'm sorry, man. She hasn't spoken to Sharlotte since Saturday. What do you want to do?"

"I'm going to give her until lunch time and then I'm going over to her job."

"Ok. Just let me know if Tara needs to make a trip up there."

"I will. Listen, I have a meeting right now, but please tell Tara to call Sharlotte. If she doesn't get her, tell her to keep trying until I can get over to her job."

"Sure thing, man. Hey, everything will be fine."

"I hope so."

I ended the call and put my phone down on my desk. I swiveled in my chair to get up and paused. *Cameras. There should be security cameras and computer logs at Sharlotte's job.*

I got up from my desk and headed for the office door. *I'll have to call in a favor on this one,* I thought.

"Ms. Simmons, please come in."

As Ms. Simmons stood to move toward my office, I noticed her thighs and toned calves. I thought of my life before Sharlotte. I would have knocked that out of the park, tore it out of the frame, laid the pipe down right and put her to sleep. Then my mind returned to Sharlotte's face when she pulled out of my driveway earlier. I replayed our conversation over and over, trying to remember what she had said about that Oldsmobile.

As Ms. Simmons walked past me to enter my office, I looked out the window of the waiting area and hoped that everything really would be ok.

Chapter Twenty-Two
The Search

"People are lazy and practical with their laziness."

Hello. It's me again. Sharlotte Swanson. You do remember me, don't you? Remember I told you from the very beginning that this love story was most important.

Well, it's coming to an end, and I'd like to be the one to tell you how it all comes out.

It was a Monday at 12:15 p.m. Lunch. JaRah, Tara and Kaisheem have made several calls all morning and into the afternoon to all the people they could think of. My clients, co-workers, family members, security officials and finally the police were notified. Kaisheem advised Tara to make preparations to head up to Maryland while JaRah called in a favor from an old college buddy who worked with Homeland Security. He arranged to go to the federal building that housed all the security tapes and authorized entry computer logs for all government agencies in D.C. JaRah sat at his desk and scribbled a few notes, then put in a call to his receptionist.

"Ms. Baker, please let my colleagues know that I'm taking the rest of the afternoon off. An emergency has come up. Reshedule my three o'clock for the next available. Would you?"

"Sure thing, Mr. Richmond. I hope that everything will be OK."

"I'm sure it will, Ms. Baker. Thank you."

JaRah hung up the phone, shut down his computer, gathered his things and headed for the door. Just as he turned the knob, his cell phone vibrated. He opened the door and paused to check the display. It was a text message from my cellular phone. He stepped outside of his office, locked the door from the inside and closed it with his left hand, while pressing buttons to view the text message with his right hand. He held his breath while he read the message:

I'm in a better place now. No need to worry
about me. Don't come looking for me. I'm
with the only one who truly loves me.

JaRah's mouth hung open. Confused and lightheaded, he looked up and around just as the room began to get dark. He saw Ms. Baker get up from her desk, saw her mouth moving and other coworkers coming toward him, but he heard no sound. He took a deep breath and felt arms holding him up, cool air being fanned in his face and several voices using words like "okay" and "cold water". Then his legs went limp and he could not get them to support his weight. He was ushered over to the waiting area and propped up in a chair.

JaRah looked past all the people in the office trying to accommodate his sudden inability to function. All he could do was stare at his phone on the floor by his office door. *Sharlotte, Sharlotte, no, no, no. Get up, go, go to her job. Get up, get it together. She didn't send that. If she did, she's ok. If she didn't someone's got her phone. Maybe they just have her phone and not her...NOT HER!*

His mind raced. His heart raced, but he was motionless. His eyes glazed over, JaRah sat motionless for what seemed like forever to him. Not a word escaped his mouth, not a blink, not so much as a heavy breath escaped from his body. Motionless, staring at his cell phone on the floor.

Someone put a cup of cool water up to his mouth. He heard voices encouraging him to drink. *Drink. Drink some water*, they suggested, but he had bigger plans. *Move, damn it MOVE! GET UP! Go find her! Now, now, NOW!*

"I have to go. I have to go now!"

JaRah eased himself up out of the chair, spilling the water that was being held up to his lips. He stood and steadied himself, his eyes still on his cell phone.

"Thank you for your help, I have to go. I'll be alright. I just have to go, NOW!"

He stood and pushed past people, walked over to his cell phone and picked it up. He felt for his car keys and left everything else exactly where it fell or had been placed.

JaRah left the office, left the people talking and asking questions, none of which he heard or responded to.

Once outside in the daylight and the fresh cold air, things seemed surreal to him. He paused as he looked across the parking lot towards *Leslie.*

He imagined my face again. He thought of me constantly, more than I ever knew.

She looked so scared this morning. Why didn't I think more of it! He hurried to Leslie, got in and started the engine. He pulled out his cell phone, went to the message and hit reply. He typed:

Where are you?

He sat for a moment and waited, waited for a reply. He looked at the clock. 2:12 p.m. He waited for a reply. Nothing. Nothing for five minutes. He put the car in reverse and headed for the federal building to review the security tapes and logs.

JaRah sped down Pennsylvania Avenue towards the Capitol, made a right on Eighth Street and rode it all the way down to Florida Avenue. He made a left on Florida Avenue and took it a few blocks down to New York Avenue. He made a right and arrived at the federal building where I worked. He pulled up to the visitor's gate and dropped the appropriate names. The gate guards made their calls and gave him a pass. They directed him to the visitor's lot and let him through.

As JaRah advanced, he noticed security vehicles patrolling the outdoor parking as well as the parking garage. Siren lights atop the security vehicle were visible from yards away.

He pulled into the visitor's lot and went to the visitor's gate. The guard read his badge and made a phone call. Minutes later, Security Specialist Marc Donnis appeared. JaRah graduated with Marc and hadn't seen him in years, but they kept in touch through email.

"JaRah! Buddy! It's good to see you again! Been years! Just wish it was under better circumstances." They shook hands and hugged.

"Yeah man. It's good to see you too. So sorry I had to trouble you like this. You know if it wasn't serious I wouldn't have."

"Oh! No trouble! This is my job!" Come with me inside; let's get to it."

The two men chatted as they entered the building and went through several more security check points before getting on the elevator. Once on the elevator, Marc Donnis scanned his employee badge and selected the ninth floor. JaRah continued to explain the situation as they ascended. The elevator doors opened and JaRah's mouth was just about dry from talking a mile a minute. They exited the elevator and JaRah spotted a water cooler not far down the hall.

"Do you mind? I need some water."

"Sure thing, buddy. Help yourself. I'm just going to check you in at the front desk, register you on the floor."

One goes left. The other goes right. A minute later they meet back in the middle.

"Come on with me this way. Let's check the logs first, see if she came in the building or logged in to any workstations."

JaRah followed Donnis's suggestion. They walked down the hall, past the water cooler and around the corner. The place seemed like a maze. They walked down several hallways, turning left, then right, and back left again. They passed cubicles filled with computer stations and people hooked up to monitors and telephones. JaRah thought to himself *I need a GPS just to get back to the elevator.*

They stopped at room 5JK098. Donnis scanned his badge on a black pad outside the door, and the latch clicked. He pushed the door open and the two walked in. The room was small and had three computers. There was one uniformed officer seated at a computer. He turned in his chair and spoke to Donnis.

"Sir, I checked the logs. Ms. Swanson's last log in was Friday evening. She logged out of her workstation at 1647. Her badge was scanned on the North elevator at 1653 and then again at the North exit at 1702. There has been no activity associated with her ID badge since then. No phone calls from her telephone or emails from her account either."

"Thank you. Good work."

Donnis opened the door and motioned for JaRah to exit as he followed behind.

"What now?" JaRah asked.

"Now we go down the hall to the north corridor and check the cameras. Most people generally park in the same area every day. We encourage folks to switch up their routines, but they hardly ever listen. See, that's where we become vulnerable creatures of habit."

"So how do you know Sharlotte parks in the north corridor?"

"That's another thing. People are lazy and practical with their laziness. I've never known anyone to park clear across the building from where they work. Inside folks tend to park close to their entrance. All the security logs are from the north corridors and north elevators, so I'm going to check the cameras in the North Corridor first."

"That makes sense. Good thing you actually know how to do your job. You know what they say about government employees."

The two share a chuckle, JaRah's first of the day. He looks at his watch, 4:34 p.m. *It will be getting dark soon. God please let her be alright. Please don't let her be scared.* JaRah and Donnis arrived at yet another door that required his badge. He scanned it. The latch clicked and with a push, the door opened to a much larger room. The two men entered and headed past cubicles and down a narrow hallway to yet another room. Donnis unlocked another door, and they entered a very cold room with huge network mainframes that lined the wall.

"This is our mainframe monitoring system for all the cameras set up on the campus. I'll start with frames from this morning around 5:30," Donnis said.

"Ok. Sharlotte left late this morning, so I would guess her arrival to be around eight on the dot, but please check as early as possible. You never know," adds JaRah.

Donnis sat down at three monitors all side by side and entered prompts into the mainframe. Freeze frames in panorama appeared. JaRah pulled up a chair and sat next to Donnis as he scrolled through them, making sure to check the time stamp and level of the parking garage on each frame. Twenty minutes into reviewing the frames, the two noticed something odd in the corner of one frame. The time stamp read 8:12 a.m. in the basement. The frame shows the tail end of an older model car and a security officer talking with the driver.

"Wait...can you go to just this camera and review the frames it took before this one?" JaRah requested.

Donnis entered more prompts into the mainframe and selected the camera, brought up all frames from the morning and went through them carefully.

JaRah shouted, "Stop! What's that? Does that look like somebody being stuffed in the trunk?"

"Let me zoom in." Donnis selected the frame an angle, then zoomed in. The two sat in amazement as they looked across all three monitors. Click. Click. Click. First frame: I was on the ground. Second frame: I was stuffed in the trunk. Third frame: the driver was stopped by security. Fourth frame, the driver was gone.

JaRah sat in disbelief with his worst nightmare confirmed. Someone had taken me. Now he realized that I was gone. JaRah pushed his chair away from the monitors and swiveled to face the wall while Donnis got on his cell phone and made some calls. *She's gone. Who took her? Who was that? Where did they go? They've been gone all day. I got that text at lunch.* Panic set in fast. JaRah jumped up out of his chair.

"Can you find the security guard who stopped that driver?"

"I'm working on that right now, buddy. Just hold tight. I'm one step ahead of you," Donnis said as he covered the receiver of his cell phone while still holding it up to his ear. JaRah paced as he thought of what to do next. *It had to be the person calling her. Maybe they work here...a janitor or a coworker, someone who knew her habits. I need to check the traffic cameras.*

"We need to check the traffic cameras!" JaRah blurted out.

"Slow down, Knight Rider! I have the vehicle information from this morning. The security guard on patrol has given the information to the police and has also given a sworn statement and description of the driver. We're running the information through our database right now. What I need for you to do is stay calm and let the authorities handle this. Come with me downstairs to the cafeteria for a hot cup of joe, then we'll head over to the main office and see what they've turned up."

Tears began to well up in JaRah's eyes. It was all beginning to sink in. I had been taken from him.

"I don't want any coffee. I want to know who that person was and where they went with my fiancée."

Donnis placed his hand on JaRah's shoulder as tear ran down his face. He scanned his badge, logged out of the mainframe and opened the door. The two left the room, made their way quietly back through the maze to the elevator and downstairs to the cafeteria. JaRah's cell phone vibrated. He pulled it out of his pocket and checked the display. It was Kaisheem. He answered reluctantly.

"Hey, man! JaRah! You there?"

"I'm here."

"You heard anything?"

"Someone took her...this morning....in the parking garage. The police got some info, but I have to wait to find out the rest."

"Man, what? Someone took her...garage...what! We're on our way. Tara took the girls to her mother's house. I turned back around to pick Tara up. She's sleeping in the passenger's seat. I don't even know what to tell her. Listen, we're in North Carolina, soon to be in Virginia. I'll call you when we get around Spotsylvania."

"Ok."

"Man, listen, just hang in there. I'm sure she's ok."

"Yeah."

"Love you, man."

"Love you too, Kaisheem. Goodbye."

END.

JaRah put his cell phone back in his pocket and looked over at Donnis. Donnis offered JaRah a cup of coffee, which JaRah declined. The two headed down the hall away from the cafeteria and through double glass doors labeled GSA. Donnis scanned his badge and they headed through yet another door into a busy office filled with both plain clothes detectives and uniformed police officers.

JaRah looked around the room at the hustle and bustle, the shuffling of paper work and ringing telephones. Crime was evident in this room.

Donnis spoke with several officers who directed him to a cubicle towards the back corner of the room. JaRah followed. Donnis introduced JaRah to the gentleman whose cubicle whose name plate read Detective Tinsley.

"JaRah Richmond, this is Detective Shawn Tinsley."

The two shook hands as Detective Tinsley spoke.

"The driver of the vehicle in question is Patricia Jones. The vehicle is registered with the Department of Motor Vehicles under her brother's name, Bradston Jones. Patricia Jones registered the vehicle here for a parking decal. Ms. Jones works here in Human Resources. We believe that's how she got Ms. Swanson's information."

Detective Tinsley continued, "We pulled Ms. Jones's computer logs and found that she accessed Ms. Swanson's personnel file on numerous occasions, beginning on Ms. Swanson's date of hire. We've put out an All Points Broadcast for the vehicle and have already sent officers to pick up her brother. He's an orderly in the psych ward over at Union City Hospital. Mr. Richmond, I assure you we are doing everything in our power to find Ms. Swanson. We just ask that you remain calm and give your full cooperation. Is there anything that you can tell us that might help us to find Ms. Swanson?"

JaRah tried to think, but his mind was blank. He hung his head and stared at his shoes. He put his hands in his pockets, felt his cell phone and thought of the text message he'd received that afternoon.

"I got a text from Sharlotte's phone...this afternoon. Her phone is a PDA. I think it has GPS. Only I don't think the text was from her. Can you use it to find the location of the phone?"

"We can certainly try. Write down her telephone number and her carrier. I'll run it over to our communications division, see what they can pull."

JaRah wrote down my telephone number on a piece of paper and fought through tears. Somewhere deep inside, he knew this was going to end horribly. He was directed to sit at a round table while waiting.

An hour later, Detective Tinsley got up from his desk, left his cubicle and came back not even two minutes later. He walked over to his chair and grabbed his jacket saying, "They got a hit off the cell phone. Come on. You two can ride with me."

JaRah wiped his face and pulled out his cell phone as Donnis, and Detective Tinsley left the office. He dialed Kaisheem's number and waited for him to answer.

"Hey? Any good news?" Kaisheem asked.

"I don't know yet. The police got a hit off Sharlotte's cell phone using GPS. I'm riding out with one of the detectives now. Where are you?'

"We're right outside of Petersburg, just about to Richmond."

"Ok. I'll call you once I know more."

"Ok? JaRah...?"

"Yeah?"

"Pray."

"Nonstop."

END.

JaRah put his phone back in his pocket and thought to himself *Someone once told me prayer should be used as the steering wheel and not the emergency brake. That has never made more sense.*

Amen, baby. I agree. Since he finally got it, I'll let him tell the rest of the story.

Chapter Twenty-Three
Discovery

"I sat up, looked around, and wondered if I had the strength to face what might be."

I sat in the back of an unmarked police cruiser, Donnis rode shot gun and Detective Tinsley drove. Blue lights sent me into a trance. City lights whizzed by and I felt like I was in a movie theater, the events of the day resembled nothing close to what my life was becoming. I closed my eyes and remembered her smell. Just this morning I held her as she cried. She was having my baby. We were going to be parents, start a family together, a life together. I blinked and blinked again, hoping the movie would soon be over, the light would come on in the theater and people around me would show themselves pleased or disappointed by the picture show.

It didn't end. I looked at the time on the radio, 7:19 p.m. This had been the longest day of my life. I hadn't eaten all day, nor did I have a desire to eat. If I could ingest anything, it would have to be the soft wetness from Sharlotte's lips. Other than that, I didn't want to bring anything towards my mouth. I looked out the window as we left city lights behind us.

"Where are we headed?" I asked.

Donnis and Detective Tinsley looked at each other in silence. Donnis looked the other way out the window and responded, "Route 1." I leaned my head back, closed my eyes and saw Sharlotte's face. Musiq Soulchild's *So Beautiful* played in my head. She loves that song, wants to dance to it at our wedding reception as our first dance. That thought brought a smile to my face and tears to my eyes all at once.

The car slowed and we made a turn off the improved roads onto a dirt gravel road. I sat up and looked around, wondering if I had the strength for what might be. I swallowed hard and put my arms up on the front seats. There were two squad cars in front of us. It was dark and I could only see what their headlights illuminated. Brake lights came on, siren lights pierced the dark. All cars pulled up to a shack and parked tactically. Officers jumped out and called for Patricia Jones to come out with her hands up.

Detective Tinsley instructed Donnis and me to stay in the vehicle as he grabbed for his gun and got out. I watched intently, every muscle in my body was tight. Donnis looked over his shoulder and told me to relax, but I couldn't. I could barely see what was going on. It was so dark. Officers scrambled with flashlights and rushed the shack, weapons drawn. I saw dust in the air through the lights. Then I saw officers shuffling back to their squad cars with their mouths covered. One officer threw up, while another was hunched over with his hands on his thighs.

"No, no, no, no! I gotta go in there! SHARLOTTE!" I screamed.

Donnis had to restrain me and Detective Tinsley eventually had to lock me in the car. I sat in the back of that car watching, one after the other go in the shack and then come out with their head in their hands. I watched and I waited. No Sharlotte, no

Patricia Jones. I screamed for someone to tell me what happened, what was going on.

Donnis walked over to the car and spoke to me through the window.

"JaRah, I'm sorry. She's gone."

"Gone? You mean, she's not in there? Where is she?"

"No JaRah. She's dead. Her throat and wrists have been cut and...and...I'm sorry, JaRah. I really am."

"I wanna see her. Let me out please."

"I can't rightfully let you see her like that. I won't do it."

"Wait for the ambulance to transport her to the hospital. Let them clean her up and sew her...You'll need to identify the body. You can see her then."

I stared into his eyes, saw into his heart. It was bad. Whatever she did to my Sharlotte, it was horrible. Donnis's eyes were glassed over. A fog from my breathe formed on the glass as Donnis backed away from the car. I sat back and tried to breath. Just then I felt my cell phone vibrate, but I couldn't move. I could barely inhale. I stared out the front glass at paramedics as they took a gurney into the shack. Then another. I couldn't wrap my mind around it. Just as soon as Sharlotte came into my life, she left it, my life, this life. She was so full of life. We were going to start a life, together and now she was dead. My cell phone vibrated in my pocket once again brought me back. I reached in, pulled it out and answered.

"We're passing Manassas. What have you found out? Where is Sharlotte? Have they found her? Is she okay?"

I couldn't speak. I was trying to answer Kaisheem, but I couldn't even fix my mouth to say it. Tears welled up in my eyes and I let out a whimper.

"JaRah! Where are you? Ok, man, just breathe."

I could hear Tara in the background asking questions and crying, becoming hysterical. I managed to find the words and say, "Dead. Both. Dead."

I heard a commotion and Tara took the phone from Kaisheem.

"Hello...hello, JaRah. This is Tara. Tell me what you just said to Kaisheem. Please!"

"I...Sharlotte...she's dead." Silence.

Then I heard it coming. I heard Tara inhale and then let out a scream that made my soul rattle. I broke down, cried so hard I couldn't hold the phone anymore. I let it fall to the seat. I curled up in a ball and just cried. I cried for what seemed like hours. I was still crying when Detective Tinsley and Donnis got back in the car and drove me to the hospital. I cried as they got me out of the backseat and I cried while the doctors tried to give me a sedative.

10:23 p.m. A hand on my shoulder, a breath on my cheek. I looked up and saw an angel, a woman whose eyes were as bloodshot as mine. She was weary and tired from travel, but still glowed with love. Just beyond her, I saw Kaisheem come through the doors of the hospital emergency room. She sat down next to me and embraced me. Her touch was soft, sweet and gentle. Her scent was light and fresh, even though she had been in a car for over 10 hours. Kaisheem sat on my opposite side. They both held me, embraced me, and covered me in love. But I was still so cold.

"JaRah, this is Tara."

186

I turned my head to look at her. She looked me in my eyes and smiled, then cried and buried her head in my shoulder. We sat there, the three of us, until the coroner came out and asked who wanted to identify the body. Tara looked at Kaisheem and me and said she can't do it.

I looked at the coroner and stood up. She motioned for me to follow her and so I did. She took me down a long hallway and through black swinging double doors, to the morgue. I followed her past several dead bodies, to a gurney in the middle of the room. She looked at the toe tag and then at me.

"Are you ok to do this right now?" she asked, and I shook my head yes as she pulled back the sheet.

Sharlotte was pale, discolored. Her hair had goops of gel in it and there were traces of smeared lipstick on her face. Her skin had already taken on a waxy appearance. There were stitches on the front of her neck, her ears, and in her hair line. I looked at her, I wanted to touch her, hold her, and apologize for not protecting her.

The coroner pulled the sheet back over her face and then looked at me and asked if I was ready to go back to the waiting room. I shook my head yes. The coroner took me by the arm and gently lead me back through the black double swinging doors and down the hall to Kaisheem and Tara.

They both looked at me like cub scouts around the camp fire, awaiting my report. Tears streamed from my eyes as I parted my cracked dry lips.

"It's her...but it's not her anymore. She's gone," I said. Kaisheem stood to comfort me, but I stepped away.

I continued, "I only knew her for eight months, but she taught me so much in that eight months. She taught me about love's truth and love's deceit. She was pregnant. We were gonna have a baby. She didn't have to let me find out, but she did. I was gonna marry her. Now she's dead, and I feel free. Completely set free because there were no lies between us. We were completely honest with each other. We never hid anything, not a thing from each other. I know that she loved me truly, without being held back by time, space or anything else that stands in the way of really loving someone."

"Man, what are you talking about?" Kaisheem was confused.

"I'm talking about you and Tara. Me and Sharlotte. I'm talking about love, true love and the truth in love. We deceive each other and try to fit love into a nice neat package, but that's not how it works. It just comes to us as is," I said.

Tara stood up and looked at me.

"I see what Sharlotte saw in you," Tara said and then turned to Kaisheem for an embrace.

As Tara and Kaisheem held each other, I made my exit out of the hospital. After reaching the parking lot, I realized that I didn't drive. I was faced with darkness. The lights from the emergency room entrance were specs.

Beyond parked cars and across a busy five lane street, life was happening and car horns were the heart beat of my moment. As the headlights from traffic put me in a daze, a bench appeared under a streetlight. I sat down and began to think about my liquid comfort awaiting me at some bar, or Mary Jane taking me on my next adventure while I was dying to be with Sharlotte. Living without her and the possibility of never finding someone new to love like I love Sharlotte hung my over head. I let my chin rest on my chest because the weight of the world was exhausting. I couldn't hold my head up.

My body was numb. The whirl of cars passing by, the occasional siren, the wind, all noise was silent. I felt the pressure on the bench beneath me shift. When I looked up, Detective Tinsley was seated next to me. He put his hand on my shoulder for comfort.

"I'm so sorry about what happened to your fiancé," Detective Tinsley said.

"I appreciate your help, Detective."

"I thought you should know that crime scene investigators set up flood lights all around that shack and found a separate set of tire marks, fresh as the set belonging to the vehicle Ms. Swanson was abducted in."

Detective Tinsley woke me up with this news. I listened attentively.

"They also dusted for finger prints and have so far found two sets. We ran the fingerprints and got two hits. One set belonged to Patricia Jones, the other set..." he paused.

My eyes wide, my lips parted, I begged Detective Tinsley not to play games with my piercing gaze as he continued,

"Bradston Jones." My blood boiled as I tried to keep from screaming.

"So you have him in custody, right? Charge him with murder!" I exclaimed.

"He has an alibi, Mr. Richmond, and we let him go an hour before the analysis came in. He's nowhere to be found."

I couldn't take it. Somebody had to go down. If this Bradston Jones was to be the one, so be it.

"Well put an APB out for him," I said.

"Mr. Richmond, we're a step ahead of you. We have units monitoring his house and the hospital where he works. My men and I will keep you posted, because this is far from over."